BEST
WOMEN'S
EROTICA
2011

BEST
WOMEN'S
EROTICA
2011

Edited by

VIOLET BLUE

CLEIS
PRESS

Published in the United States by Cleis Press, Inc., 2246 Sixth Street, Berkeley, California 94710.

Printed in the United States.
Cover design: Scott Idleman
Cover photograph: Adri Berger/Getty Images
Text design: Frank Wiedemann
Cleis Press logo art: Juana Alicia
First Edition.
10 9 8 7 6 5 4 3 2 1

ISBN: 978-1-57344-423-1

CONTENTS

INTRODUCTION:
MELTED

This 2011 edition of *Best Women's Erotica* is stylish, coy, slick with gloss and stiletto sharp: desirous, dangerous; ice cream in the heat; love lost and found again; filthy with laughter. This year, something changed.

Whether shy or brazen, we all seem to be seeking our melting point more than ever before. I'm watching it happen faster than culture can deal with it. That we still hear messages about women not liking any one kind of sex until we really examine it for ourselves, implies a world of dizzying contradictions we'd just as soon burn down as bend over for. Tell us we don't like explicit sexual fantasy, and we'll booby-trap your pedestal of female desire with nitroglycerin.

Our fantasies are indeed about fucking, not shopping. No passive accessories for another person's sex life, we've become erotically ambitious, down to the last woman. This globally sourced collection of stories from top female erotic writers takes this point of view for granted. As the editor, I had to bow to this iconoclastic trend. Writers are pulse points for culture; women have moved away from what we are "supposed" to get turned on by, to seek (and demonstrate) what we really want.

What happened? We grew accustomed to erotic anthologies that almost apologized for women having the temerity to say they had fantasies that gave them hard-ons. Mainstream publishers still crank out tepid oatmeal erotica thinking that aiming for the middle—looking away from the real female gaze—is the way to stay safe. Meanwhile indies like Cleis Press, run by women, have fostered a powerfully quiet revolution, upending the market-place by the simple act of giving women what they want.

When did we first reject the notions that our vaginas are dirty and we should not speak out of turn? It actually happened very gradually, as one generation grew into another, and as girls real-ized we could be anyone we wanted to online, look at anything we wanted to. Men have a free pass to jerk off to porn outside the relationship; women suddenly wanted to know, why don't we? We discovered that sexual fantasy wasn't just a thing to try once or twice; it was something that was *necessary*. The stories I got sent every year started to change. They became more direct.

Stories sent to me when I post a call for submissions arrive in the hundreds from all over the world, and in my ten years of editing erotica, these stories always tell me what's going on out there in people's heads about sex, specifically, women's heads. Culture bleeds themes into the stories, and I'll often get multiple takes on any given pop culture topic or timely sex act, the authors each having no idea that their stories are part of a trend. This year, for instance, it was looking at pornography. Women owning the right to look. At the same time, suddenly this year every single story is layered top to toe with explicit sex, hard and wet and mean and sweet, flowing around love, and fused with characters who finally feel like us, with no apologies.

This collection is ice cream at its best moment: melting in the heat.

Sure, these authors and their sexual heroines have some cool sweets. But the negligee they're wearing for seduction is soaked in gasoline, and like a sexily perverse scene out of *Mad Men,* these women all want a light.

In Louisa Harte's "Changing My Tune" we begin with a warm breeze by the seaside, where a girl squeezed into a tight uniform has her first day on the job serving ice cream to workmen—with no small amount of irony about her presentation. That is, until she sees a way to capitalize on her situation to get off in two tense encounters that merge the thrill of getting caught with being romanced by one of the hard-bodied boys. The next show is in Chrissie Bentley's "Pictures of Lilly," where a group of girls finally dare to see what it's like in the male-only arena of a triple-X movie theater. Sneaking into the dark enclave mixes the girls' erotic fright with sexual wonder. The hard-core visuals and arousal become so acute that one of the girls steps through the looking glass in a way that surprises, but feels like it must be based on a true story.

Upon reading "Two for One," by Alyssa Turner, I felt a deep envy and a burning wish that this could happen to me, too, and make those times spent traveling to conventions and hotels as filled with sexual possibility as it must be for men. In it, a businesswoman splurges on spa service in her hotel room, only to be confronted by two masseurs who compete to see which can give her the most physical pleasure to win the payment, and tip.

"I, Anita," by Lana Fox is striking fare—a fantasy so delicious, vivid, debauched and ripe, it could easily be adapted to film. Anita is a sleek, corseted burlesque dancer whose act includes conjuring male orgasms onstage, saving her sexual release only for herself—until she meets the Baron, and all bets are off as bodice-ripping becomes nail-raking orgasms. Amelia Thornton's "Chlorine" echoes a similar mood of timelessness and evokes languid afternoon perversions á la Nabokov's *Lolita,* when a wealthy benefactress's mysterious young companion steps out of line at an elite hotel poolside.

It's possible you may have heard of "rainbow parties," but in "Rainbow Night," by Giselle Renarde, a group of high-class couples at a dinner party not only discuss the ritual of a man collecting as many colors of lipstick as he can on his willing member, but in a scene of high erotic tension, devise a way to try it for dessert. Speaking of leaving no one out, erotica luminary Donna George Storey cranks up the taboo and the heat when a powerful businesswoman uses social media to create a multi-partner sex scene where she is the "Fresh Canvas" for men who come for *her* pleasure.

No stranger to transgression is star author Cecilia Tan, whose story shows from sentence number one why she's a luminary—while making us laugh and turning us on at the same time. In "Two Cocks, One Girl," a woman with good-natured snark explores her boyfriend's emerging interest in cock. This interest handily matches her own and culminates in fresh sexual encounters and a creative cure for joblessness.

An increasingly favored author brings her talent to the collection: the imitable Jacqueline Applebee. In "Skinheads," the gifted UK author blends life as a young black woman raised in a London ghetto with a cultivated fetish for a certain kind of boy who wears Doc Martens. It's a gritty and unsettlingly arousing encounter that she orchestrates like a sexed-up conductor, wringing delicious domination with a strap-on. Another force to reckon with, writer Valerie Alexander takes us into *"King Slut,"* the imaginary porno world of a woman whose fantasies—like many of ours—play better as the porno movie in her mind than the stuff everyone around her wants to watch. Meanwhile, her crush object finally ends the guessing game of whether or not he's interested, shockingly becoming the masked star of her pornographic dreams.

If you've ever been on New York streets and felt the pull of a hot chance encounter, then Louise Lagris's "I Wish You Were Braille" won't leave your mind anytime soon after you've read it. Even if you're not familiar with the city, when the heroine finally connects with a certain tattooed boy in a bar and then enjoys strangely powerful sex tempered by impossible longing, like me, you may find it difficult to forget. "Picture Me Naked," by Velvet Moore, is another outstanding piece of writing based in a bustling city, where a woman turns the humiliation of an ex-boyfriend exposing a naked picture of her to the world into her own private game; leaving a masturbatory trail of dirty self-portraits across the cityscape—with unintended results.

Unintended results are exactly what the jealous roommate in celebrity author Alison Tyler's "Want" has on her hands. The problem is, her annoying roommate's boyfriend makes her an offer she can't refuse—erotic punishment of the roommate, but only in exchange for something very filthy that she herself has never tried, but always wanted. Cascading into the edge of filthy fantasy and just beyond is "Tricks," by Lola Olson, which offers up one of the most intense tales of the collection. In it, a woman acts out her fantasy of dressing up as a street hooker for a sexual takedown by beat cops, the twist coming (as does she) when he "calls for backup."

Far from the gritty city is a tale so iconic and compelling that it blurs the line of contemporary explicit erotica and mythology: "Sealskin," by Kirsty Logan, unfolds on a quiet Isle of Skye nighttime beach. Sirens? Quite possibly, of the female lesbian kind for sure, though this story ultimately feels like an arousing fever dream. Also dreamlike but packed with erotic thrill, Cynthia Hamilton's "Opportunity" depicts a lesbian protagonist who is presented with a blindfolded surprise for her birthday: her girl-friend gifting her sex with a man—for her very first time.

This collection is not short on famous names in the erotica genre, and Sommer Marsden shines in a slightly dark female sexual fantasy, "Laps." In this story a female athlete has more than a sexual relationship with her trainer, finding absolution in moments when she will literally do anything to please him, including sex in public.

Not only famous in erotic writing, Rachel Kramer Bussel is an online media sensation. In one of the most powerful stories I've ever read, "Espionage" seems to pull from a very deep place to create a story I've returned to more than once. Here, we are the girl at the party who's been having a torrid affair with the man of the house, seeing his wife for the first time as guests float in and out and finally mustering up the force to do something that dares him to be ours, even if just for that one intense moment that rips our fishnets.

Closing the curtain is a legendary name I swooned over in my first forays into erotica: Janine Ashbless showed me that erotica can be literature, and in "Abigail's Ice Cream" we get another helping of the sublime, slippery dessert we started out with. As you sink into the world of a gourmet ice-cream maker, you'll also get a taste of the endless possibilities presented to a single woman running her own business—dishing up treats at a festival alongside hunky paramedics who tease and play with both sweets and the sweet life. A sweet life that happens to include delicious multipartner (multiflavor?) trysts, that is.

Now, find something that melts, and turn up the heat.

Violet Blue
San Francisco, California

CHANGING MY TUNE

Louisa Harte

"Two large cones, please, love."

I glance over the counter at the sweaty builder. He points up at the menu on the side of the van, but his eyes are fixed on my tits, barely concealed within my ridiculously tight uniform.

"Sure, coming right up," I say sweetly, giving him my best professional smile. It'd be funny if I hadn't already heard that joke about ten times today. Still, I'm easy pickings—whoever designed these uniforms must be having a laugh. With their tight zipper-front top and barely there skirt, they wouldn't look out of place in a kinky costume shop. But it's not my place to argue. I pick up the scoop and start preparing the ice creams.

This job sure isn't what it's cracked up to be. When I signed up, I thought I'd be cruising about in a flash ice-cream van serving up goodies and treats to crowds of eager customers. Instead, while others in the fleet get to go to big gigs and fancy festivals, I end up here, on a beach in the middle of nowhere, next to a building site.

Typical.

"There you go." I hand over the ice creams. The builder drops the change into my hand before giving me a leery wink and swaggering back off to his mates.

I sigh. If the obscenely tight uniform and crappy pink van weren't bad enough, the trashy jingle I've got playing is enough to set my teeth on edge. I lean over and switch it off—that's enough of "Greensleeves" for now. Still, this job is only for the summer and it does have its pluses. I gaze down at the colorful assortment of ice creams and my mouth starts to water.

"Hello, love." A voice calls my attention. I look up. It's another builder, only this one is different—he's gorgeous. Like a hot builder from an advert on TV, he has these sexy gray eyes, gorgeous red lips and a rocking body that looks great packed into his T-shirt and shorts. I can almost smell the pheromones coming off him.

"Oh, hi," I say. Am I blushing? "What can I get you?"

The guy rests his arm on the counter and gazes up at the menu. "What do you recommend?"

I stifle a smile. Is he serious? This is an ice-cream van, not the Ritz. Still, it gives me a chance to have a bit of fun. "I hear the raspberry ripple's rather nice…" I hold my breath. It's a challenge—offering a big tough builder a rather girly sounding ice cream.

He takes it. "Right, the ripple it is."

I try to hide my delight as I scoop his ice cream. I like a man who's up for a laugh. Especially one this hot.

"What's your name?" he asks, watching me as I prepare his ice cream.

"Cassie," I say, a little surprised. Punters aren't usually interested in details like that.

"Cassie. Hmm. I like that," he says, with no trace of irony.

"Nice to meet you, Cassie. I'm Luke."

Polite, too. I'm impressed.

"There you go, Luke." I hand over his ice cream. "Hope you enjoy it."

Luke drops the coins into my palm. "I'm sure I will." He gives me a knowing smile before ambling off to a nearby bench to sit and eat.

I watch him, intrigued. There's something unusual about him. He doesn't just wolf his ice cream down like the others—he takes his time; savors it, eats it slowly like it's a treat to be relished.

And, oh, how he eats it.

I lean against the counter, my jaw going slack at the spectacle on display. First he rolls his tongue around the outside of the ice cream, coating his tongue in the creamy mixture. Then he draws it into his mouth with long luscious laps that look really suggestive. At least they do to my dirty mind. I lean forward to get a better look.

Next he starts nibbling and licking—deft precise movements that have me quaking at the knees. He's seducing that dessert like it's a succulent pussy. I can't help but react. My nipples harden against the front of my top, and I feel my own creamy moisture start to seep into my panties. Is he doing this for me? Though the thought seems ridiculous, it gets me excited, and I watch him even closer, drawn in by his erotic food play. I'm glad there's no queue. At last someone up there loves me.

Luke turns his attention to the crisp little cone. He holds it gently and starts to nibble it with precise little nips that look calculated to please. And they do. I press my thighs together, my pussy getting wetter at the sight.

After a few more bites, he finishes the ice cream. But the show isn't over. I watch, engrossed as Luke licks his fingers, one by one, draining every last trace of ice cream from them.

I let out a sigh. Wow, that was hot.

Suddenly, Luke gets up and starts ambling back toward the van. I snatch up a scoop, pretending to be busy.

Luke rests his arm on the counter. "Hey, thanks for that, Cassie, I really enjoyed it."

"Yeah, so did I." Oh, hell, did I say that out loud?

Luke tips his head, a smile on his face. "Right, well. Maybe see you later?" Before I can reply, he strolls away, back to the building site.

I take a few deep breaths. My palms are sweaty, my knickers are soaking. I feel like I've been watching a filthy movie, the way my body's reacting. I gaze over at the ice creams and realize I'm in no fit state to serve anyone—except myself.

A sly smile crosses my lips. That's it. There's nothing else for it. I'll close the van, give myself a quick seeing to and get this thing out of my system. I grasp the serving window to slide it closed, but then an elderly guy wanders over. "Hold on love, I need some relief out here, I'm melting," he says.

I grimace, pressing my thighs together beneath my tight skirt. *Yeah? You and me both.* Still, I put on my professional smile and get to work. Perhaps keeping busy will take my mind off my arousal. But as I scoop the ice cream, my mind fills with images of Luke, nibbling that cone like it was my pussy. My hands start to shake. I deserve an award just for keeping a straight face with all the kinky images passing through my mind. But somehow I manage to keep my cool and serve up the ice cream.

"Thanks, love." The guy saunters off down the beach to enjoy his treat.

Right. Time for mine.

I can't get the window closed fast enough. Clearing a space on the floor in the back of the van, I lie down next to freezers of prepackaged Popsicles and ruck up my skirt. Sliding my hand into my knickers I run my fingers over my slit, swirling them in my juices. I moan and tip my head back against the floor. Damn, I feel horny. Hand in my knickers, I pant and groan as I rub myself up.

My moans echo off the walls—I sound far too conspicuous. I've always been a noisy lover and I need something to cover my reactions. I scramble up and flick the switch on the music. As the tinny sound of "Greensleeves" cranks up, I scrabble back down onto the floor and get back to the job. I never thought I'd be wanking to "Greensleeves," but I guess, right now, the jingle does have its uses.

I tease and rub my clit between my fingers, picturing Luke's head between my thighs, lapping and sucking. I roll my head from side to side and murmur, the tremors inside me increasing. Just a few more strokes and I'll be there…

There's a knock on the window. I groan and sit up, woozy from the preorgasmic sensations. There it is again, more insistent this time. I sigh. In this business, the customer always comes first.

How bloody ironic.

I tug my skirt back down over my legs and straighten my hat. Stumbling up off the floor, I dash over to the window and slide it open.

It's Luke. "Hey, gorgeous. I heard the music and I thought you were open…."

Hell, I'd forgive him anything. "Sure. What do you fancy?" *A kiss, a grope, a seriously good fuck in the van?*

Luke tilts his head and looks thoughtful. "I'm after something a bit indulgent…."

"Yeah, like what?" I lean over the counter, breath held, expectant.

Luke leans in to meet me. "Something soft and juicy with a

hint of cream." He runs his gaze over my body. "Do you have anything like that?"

There's no mistaking the hint. His eyes, his words—his whole manner says, *fuck me*. My head fills with all kinds of naughtiness. Who am I to deny this hot customer his wish? I run my fingers over the counter, a coy smile on my face. "I think I know what you're after, but I'll have to serve it to you in the back of the van…"

Luke meets my gaze. "Sounds perfect."

My fingers fumble as I slide the window shut for the second time. I know I risk losing my job with all these impromptu closures, but one look at Luke's luscious red lips and there's no going back. I can't get to the back of the van fast enough.

I open the door. Luke stands in front of me, all manly and oozing sexuality. The filthy look on his face gets me right to the core. I can't resist. Doing a quick check for onlookers, I grab hold of his T-shirt and pull him into the van. Luke slams the door closed behind us. In the compact space, his brawny body looks even bigger, even more enticing. Moving closer, he puts his arm around my waist and edges me back against the freezers. "So, this special indulgence…"

With a cheeky smile, I slide the zipper down on my top. "It's all right here—help yourself.…"

Luke's eyes sparkle as my tits spill out into his hands. "Mmm, just as I pictured, two big scoops of ice cream." He runs his fingers around their contours, his rough hands surprisingly sexy against my skin. "Topped off with a couple of pert raspberries." He flicks his thumbs over my nipples. "And what's this?" Luke slides his hand under the hem of my skirt and cups my wet pussy. "A generous smothering of cream…"

I moan and thrust my crotch into his palm. The guy's a whiz with the sex talk, but any more of this teasing and I'll go crazy.

I tilt his chin up to face me. "Just quit with the sweet talk and shut up and eat me."

Luke chuckles. "Yes, ma'am." Whipping off my panties, he grabs my ass and sets me down on top of the freezers. Kneeling between my spread thighs, he lifts my legs over his shoulders and buries his face in my pussy.

I gasp. The kinky display he put on earlier was no smoke screen—the guy is as good as his promise. Looking up at me with those deep gray eyes, he rolls his tongue over my slit in long slow strokes before spearing it into my cunt. I wriggle, enjoying the contrast of the cold freezers against my ass and his hot tongue in my pussy. Luke slides his hands over my thighs and trails his tongue over my clit, starting a heady rhythm over the tip. I grip the edge of the freezers and groan. He's putting on a show again—only this time it's me that he's eating. I rock my hips to meet him as he licks, sucks and fucks me with his mouth. He pushes first one finger, then another into my cunt to add to the thrill. I whimper and run my fingers through his hair. He's misplaced on that building site; his talent belongs here, eating pussy.

As he continues to nuzzle and suck me, I get tingles all over my body. Luke flicks his tongue faster, coaxing me to orgasm. *Oh, yeah, here it is.* I grab a handful of his hair and clench my thighs as I come in his face.

Luke looks up at me with those dark eyes and licks the juice from my pussy. He trails his fingers over my slit one last time before placing my legs back down onto the floor and getting to his feet. Meeting my gaze, he slides his fingers one after the other into his mouth to lick off my juices. Then he leans back against the wall, a satisfied smile on his face. "Thanks for that, Cassie, I really enjoyed it."

This time there's no reticence in my reply. "Yeah, so did I." I gaze at him, the hot, burly builder with the tongue from heaven, and I feel excitement build all over again. My gaze dips lower and I see his thick cock tenting his shorts and I can't let him go. Not yet. Not without a taste of him.

I push myself up off the freezers and sidle toward him. "That was great, but I think we forgot something...."

Luke tips his head.

I grab a bottle of chocolate sauce off the side. "What good's an ice cream without a nice juicy topping..." Before he can move, I drop to my knees and whip his shorts down to his ankles. Luke looks down at me, surprised. Hooking my hands in the waistband of his boxers, I drag them down over his thighs, he steps out of shorts and boxers, and I toss them both aside. The look in Luke's eyes grows more serious. Released from its constraints, his cock springs forward into my face. I kneel level with it, admiring the sight—hard and thick, it's a thing of beauty.

I lick my lips. I'm going to enjoy this.

Luke groans and shifts his weight back against the wall as I drizzle sauce over his cock. Tossing the bottle onto the counter, I kneel back to examine my handiwork. Chocolate-covered cock: I like it. I lean in and flick my tongue over his shaft, lapping up the sexy sauce. Luke's face contorts. He bucks his hips, trying to drive himself into my mouth. "Patience," I whisper. I stroke his balls and lick the head of his cock, taking time to tease him. But my resolve doesn't last long—he's far too tasty to toy with. Wrapping my lips around the tasty treat, I swallow him.

Luke groans. I pump my head up and down over his prick taking him deeper and deeper, the taste of chocolate and his salty flesh mingling in my mouth. I gaze up at Luke's agonized expression and there's no stopping me. Down on my knees on the van floor, my skirt still rucked up around my waist, I suck on his huge prick, getting hotter and hornier by the second. Oh, boy, do I want him.

As if he can tell, after a few swift strokes, Luke threads his hands in my hair and pulls back, withdrawing his cock from my mouth. He gazes down at his cock, now slick with my saliva, then cheekily at me. "Hey, Cassie, what's a cone without a nice juicy place to stick it...?"

My legs quiver. This cheesy banter is getting me off and I almost fall over myself in an effort to get to my feet. Luke smirks at my eagerness. Lifting me up, he perches me against the edge of the freezers and tears off his T-shirt. Wow. Hard, lean and muscular—the guy looks amazing. But it's his thick purple cock that has my mouth watering.

Luke moves to stand between my spread thighs. He slides his hands under my ass and lifts me against him. "You sure about this?" he rasps.

I wrap my legs around his waist. *You bet.* I lean back against the freezers and tilt my hips up toward him. "Bring it on."

Luke surges forward driving his huge prick inside me. I arch my back, and cry out. Hard and filling, he sure feels satisfying buried in my cunt. I gaze down at my breasts jiggling as he starts to pound into me. This is bliss. Supporting me with one arm, he reaches for the chocolate sauce and drizzles it over my tits. He leans forward and sucks chocolate from my nipples, all the while working his cock into my pussy. I gaze up at the ceiling and sigh. I never thought working in the ice-cream van could be this much fun.

Luke throws his head back. "Man, you're hot," he murmurs, his lips trembling as he pistons his hips up against me.

I thrust my hips back to meet him. "You're not so bad yourself."

We heave and buck, cupboards rattling, thighs slapping and groans ringing out. I'm not sure even "Greensleeves" can cover this onslaught. But this time, I don't care—all joking aside, this is one seriously good fuck. I reach down between my thighs and give my clit a good rub, feeling the orgasm approaching.

Luke's thrusts increase. I tighten my legs around his muscled back and slam back against him—I'm getting closer and closer to the brink. *Oh, hell, this is it.* My pussy contracts. I groan, my body convulsing in a huge juicy climax. One more thrust, and Luke cries out too. He turns his head to the side and buries his face against my breasts as he spurts himself into my pussy.

I lie back against the freezers, Luke still nestled between my thighs. I lift my head to look at him. "That was amazing." I stroke my hands through his hair, a dazed expression on my face.

Luke lifts his head. "Yeah, it was." He strokes his hands over my tits and looks thoughtful. "Only, I don't know about you, but I'm still hungry...."

I smile. "Yeah, me too." I pull him in for a kiss, feeling his hot lips burn me up all over again.

Suddenly, there's a knock on the van window.

Oh hell—a customer.

I wiggle my hips trying to slide out from underneath Luke. "I have to go."

Luke clasps my waist. "Can't they wait?"

I falter at the pleading look in his eyes. "Yeah, okay, why not." I grab his head and pull his lips back down onto mine.

"Cassie!"

I feel the color drain from my cheeks.

"What's the matter?" Luke says.

My voice comes out in a whisper. "It sounds like Max—my boss."

The next few minutes are a blur as we scramble around the van trying to put our clothes back on. I've only just straightened my hat when the voice calls out again—"Cassie, are you in there? What's going on?"

"I'll be right there." I usher Luke to the back of the van and then sprint to the window to open it.

"Max...what a nice surprise," I say, gazing down at the agitated face of my boss.

"I just stopped by to see how things were going and I find you're all shut up. And it's peak time too. What's the problem?" he says.

"Um..." I flex my fingers trying to come up with a good excuse.

"Actually, it's my fault."

My heart almost stops beating as I turn to see Luke standing beside me.

"Your wonderful operative here has been kind enough to give me a personal tour of the van," Luke continues, sounding very self-assured.

Max's eyes narrow. "Oh, yes—and you are?"

"Luke Forewright of Forewright Construction Company."

I gape. I don't know who looks more surprised—me or Max.

Max's expression softens, but he still looks suspicious. "Now then, Cassie, you know you aren't supposed to let people into the van."

"Yeah, I know, but..." I gaze down at the counter as if I'll find the answer there.

Thankfully, Luke steps in to rescue me. "I'm considering making a business proposition, and I wanted to see firsthand the variety of refreshments on offer."

I raise my brows at that one.

Max looks intrigued. "And?"

Luke slides his hand under my skirt and gives my ass a squeeze. "Very tasty."

I shiver. The cheeky...

Luke continues. "So tasty in fact that I'd like to ask if you'd consider posting this van here for the rest of the summer...."

Max's eyes flash. I can see the dollar signs there.

"My men certainly work up an appetite," Luke continues, circling my buttocks.

"Well, that does sound promising." Max turns his attention to me. "What do you think, Cassie?"

I slide my hand over Luke's crotch and do a little squeezing of my own. "Yeah, I guess it could work out."

"Well, then, that's settled," Max says.

Luke steps down off the van and gives Max a polite handshake. "Right, I'll be off then," he says, turning to me. "See you tomorrow, Cassie."

I catch the glint in his eye. "You bet." I watch him stroll back to the building site, a fuzzy glow in my chest.

Max puts his arm around my shoulder. "I must say, Cassie, I never knew you had such good business acumen."

I smile back at him sweetly. Neither did I.

A few minutes later and I'm heading out of the parking lot in my little pink van, a huge smile on my face. If I'm not careful I'll even be humming "Greensleeves."

I WISH YOU WERE BRAILLE

Louise Lagris

This city is never small enough when you want it to be, but sometimes you circle the same people for years until your Venn diagrams bump into each other by accident. Later we tried to pinpoint how we'd managed to accidentally avoid each other so neatly but could never decide, chalking it up instead to a trickster god who gets his jollies from fucking with the good people of New York City.

But sometimes the planets configure themselves into origami shapes that bring me to my knees with joy at this city, and tonight was one of them. Because I dragged myself out to a bar to meet friends who brought friends, and somehow there was that fellow with the ink-picked heart on the side of his throat I'd been passing on the street for as long as I'd lived here. I never had a reason to say hi, no eye contact, just me looking at him with knives in my eyes, hoping he'd look back. But introductions were made and somehow my karma clicked into place for once, and Joe and I spent the evening slipping quarters into the jukebox, play-arguing over who has better taste in music, playing Echo and the Bunnymen, Buzzcocks, Joy Division, the bands on all the old T-shirts we had in our ancient collections.

Things were nice, warm, fuzzy. I felt like I was in a warm bath or soft pajamas, not a bar drowned in red lights with a movie screen playing *Barbarella* at our backs. We didn't talk of anything important—our families, where we went to high school or college, what our ideal jobs were—we just played around and laughed and I really wanted to go home with him.

So tipsily, gigglingly, giddily, that's what I did.

"I have to walk my dog," he said. "Do you want to meet her? She's sort of my litmus test, you see."

"What will she do if she doesn't approve?"

"Nothing, just ignore you. But being ignored by Miss Sugarpig is like being ignored by the Pope. It cuts deep."

"I think I can handle it," I said and finished my drink.

We weren't drunk per se, but loosey-goosey as you are when you've drunk just enough to be silly, because you drink faster when you're nervous than when you're not. I tripped over invisible cracks in the sidewalk and girlishly clutched his arm. I could feel the wiry muscles underneath his leather coat and long-sleeve shirt, which only allowed the smallest peeks of his tattoos, which made them all the more titillating, like the glimpse of a Victorian ankle or petticoat. We sang Richard Hell songs as we walked through Tompkins Square Park, where homeless punks slept next to the cement chess stands and squirrels stared ludicrously from ancient tree branches that survived the squatter riots.

Joe lived on the fourth floor of a five-floor walkup on Avenue C. The stairs were narrow, and I got a splinter from the railing. He walked behind me, and I blushed with the feeling of his eyes on my ass but wiggled a little extra at the same time, flushed all over. I was already wet.

I flattened myself against the wall so he could unlock the door. We were both panting a little from the walk, but also from nervousness; at least I was. My teeth chattered and a few tremors went down my back as he opened the door and we went in.

Sugarpig was waiting at the door; she nosed his knee and, I swear, motioned her head toward the door like, "Come on, come on, get the leash and let's go." He nudged her back, gently, with his knee.

"Sorry, Shug, go lie down."

"But, ah, I thought we were going to walk her?"

"Ah, well, see...that was kind of not true. I walked her before I left." He was looking at the dog, who had settled herself on her dog bed in the corner. She huffed. She was shining white in the light from the windows, her pink nose moist and candylike, her eyes sizing me up. She was indeed a formidable presence, one that I would have to win over should this one night turn into more.

"You're not mad, are you?"

"No, of course I'm not."

"Echo, my cat, is hiding. She gets jealous."

"Sorry, Echo-echo-echo..." His mouth stopped me from this goofiness. I laughed into it and felt his wide lips smile on mine. His mouth was a little chapped but gentle; when I responded to his kisses with a tiny, tiny bite on his lower lip, it unlocked something in him that he'd been holding back and he bit me back harder. His tongue went in my mouth deeper, and I turned my head so he could lick my neck and ear. He pulled on my earrings, and I giggled. He stuck his nose in my ear, and I pulled away, and he pulled me back. Tug of war, the kind you have on playgrounds.

He was taller than he looked; I had to stand on the balls of my feet and crane my head to kiss him and totally failed when I tried to nip at his neck. He put his hands on my shoulders and, still kissing me, led me over to the couch and gently pushed me over. Very gently, as if I was a vase he wanted to tip over, but he was scared he would get in trouble for breaking it. I let myself fall, and when he climbed on top of me I threw my legs around him and nearly kicked over the end table with my boots. His hips were narrow between my thighs; his belt buckle dug into my stomach. I think we kissed and wriggled and play-humped for an hour, like teenagers. His hands were delicious, long fingered with rounded fingernails, and his body was boyish above me.

Suddenly Joe stood up and held out his hand.

"Shall we?" he asked, like we were elegantly dressed ball-room dancers in a '50s movie.

"Yes. Yes, we shall." I took his hand.

A streetlight glowed from behind the gauzy curtains. The bed was rumpled and slept-in; a tiny calico cat was snuggled up in one of the mounds of sheets. She saw us, yawned and ran into the closet.

Joe took off my glasses and carefully put them on the end table. I lay back on the bed, and he took one of my boots in his hands, gently unlacing it and pulling it off and dropping it on the floor, then running his hand up my leg. He kissed the inside of my knee, and I felt it all the way up. Then he did the same for my other boot. I shivered.

I sat up and kissed him hard; part of my brain wanted to take a chunk out, consume him, chew him up and swallow. We knelt on the bed facing each other. Finally I could reach his ears, his neck; I ran my tongue in the hollows of his collarbone and followed the thumping vein in his neck up to the back of his ear. His hands were all over me, under my clothes, on top of them, like they were another layer of skin that felt just as good to touch as my bareness underneath. I licked and kissed his neck.

"Did it hurt?" I whispered.

"It hummed and throbbed," he whispered back. "Like singing or an operation. An intubation. I don't know. Maybe like this?"

He took the front of my throat in his mouth, worrying it with his teeth, thrumming his tongue right on my voice box. I laughed.

"That's it," he whispered. "That's just how it was. But not nearly as nice. Wish you had been the one tattooing me."

"I can't draw."

"You can draw on me."

"When?"

"Now."

"No, right now, I want to see what else you have drawn on you." I unbuttoned his shirt and pulled it off, and he sat there half in shadows, the illustrated man, one I could touch, and I did. I started with the heart on his throat and traced the line down to his chest; he was nearly hairless except for a few hairs curling around his nipples. The caps of his shoulders were covered with dotted Tibetan clouds and wind; I walked on my knees around him to inspect his back, which took my breath away. It was a giant scene of clouds and flowers, spirals and vines of dots, thousands and thousands of dots. The flowers were the only parts with color, pale pinks that shimmered like watercolors I could barely see in the semidark. I expected to feel the dots raised under my fingers like Braille and was disappointed to feel it was mostly like skin; I wanted to read him, I wanted to feel the needle marks like signs from God.

I massaged the tops of his shoulders, his solid deltoids, the muscles in his back that flexed beneath my fingers, beneath their illustrations. I kissed each flower and spiral, each cloud and vine.

I walked back around to his front and smiled.

"There's nowhere else to draw on you," I whispered.

"What about you?"

"My skin is plain. There are plenty of places to draw on."

"You are anything but plain," he said, his hands at the hem of my shirt, his fingers playing with and touching my belly. His hands hesitated, so I kissed him and he continued raising my shirt, and I held my arms up so he could pull it over my head. I sat back, my knees beginning to go numb, and he looked at me fully. He ran his hands up and down my arms, my belly, my sides, trickled his fingers down my breasts. I reached behind me and undid my bra, dropped it to the floor, resisted the temptation to cross my arms in front of me. We kissed, naked chest to naked chest, our hands touching each other's backs and sides. I pushed him down this time, gently, a tiny, half-naked lumberjack whispering *timber*. I lay on top of him, told him to stay still and kissed his chest up and down, his nipples and navel, the born-again soft skin just below his armpits. I touched the hair there wonderingly, thinking about how I used to stare at the boys when they raised their hands in sixth grade, waiting for the tiniest peek of fine hair to escape from their shirtsleeves. This part of the men I've been with never seems to age past then, or else just seeing it still awes me, reminds me I'm a grown-up and I can see the secret, finely haired places of men any time I want. I gently stuck a finger beneath the waist of his jeans, and he sucked in his stomach to invite me in.

This is when things always speed up. Should I savor this half-naked exploration, make it last, the revelations of skin inch by inch? His erection was distorting his jeans; when I put my hand on it, he gasped and rubbed against me. I fell on him, and together we ground our pelvises together, knocking bone and bone, jeans and jeans, pinching nipples and biting lips and ears and necks. He scratched my back with invisible nails. Finally I began fumbling with his belt buckle, and he sat back and whipped it off, threw it on the floor, unbuttoned the first button of his jeans and there was his cock, hot and dark pink and gaspingly escaped from the waist of his boxers, lying against the trail of fine hairs running down from his shallow navel. He paused—what was he thinking? Trying to decide if he wanted to continue, or was he embarrassed, or was it something else altogether? But he continued; he raised himself to his knees and unzipped his jeans, wiggled them down and lay down next to me to take them off.

I was the more clothed one for once. So many times the guy still has on his clothes, maybe his jeans or pants, maybe all of his clothes, while I lie back naked and cold, waiting for them to lie on me and warm me up. Instead, he was skinny and naked, stippled with ink on his back and arms and even, I saw, his thighs. Skinny like a boy you want to feed, skinny like my first boyfriend in seventh grade.

He stuck his hand down my jeans and inhaled quickly when he felt how wet I was, how soaked. He brought his fingers to his mouth and licked them; he kissed me and his mouth tasted like my cunt, and he stuck his index finger in my mouth and that tasted like my cunt too. I bit his finger and took his hand and put it down my jeans again.

"Two, three, four," I told him. More fingers. More. He bundled them up and worked them inside me like a small dick. I curved up into his hand, rocking and flexing, until I came with a flood and a rush and he licked his fingers again.

He scooched down the bed until his nose was level to the button on my jeans. He licked my belly button. He gently bit the curve of belly beneath. He licked just beyond the waist of my jeans, where it was dark and hot, and I was still radiating heat from his finger fuck.

He bit at the brass button closing my jeans. I giggled, my stomach rippling above him. I wished I loved him, I wished I knew who he was, but mostly I just wished he'd take off my jeans and lick my pussy and quit fucking around with the button.

Which he did.

He bit and worried and licked the flesh around my hips, on the inside of my thighs, where my torso met my legs. He breathed on my cunt but refused to get nearer, ducking away when I strained toward him. He was rubbing his cock on the bed, on the mounds of sheets, he was gasping his hot breath right on me but still not touching. Oh, he knew what he was doing. He didn't read this in some lad mag. Someone taught him; he learned from practice and from the love of it. A woman can tell when someone doesn't want to go down on her, but he was already there. He put his whole mouth on my clothed vulva; the shock of warmth made me hiss unintelligible pleas. I could feel him smile. Then I felt the impossibly soft, wet touch of his tongue nudging my panties aside—first on the left, then on the right, licking me up and down, nipping each lip, slipping his tongue under the cloth still covering my slit. I wanted to throw something at him; I wished he had long hair so I could grab it and pull him in. He slipped his fingers in and pulled them away from me, nosed in and licked. Choking sounds came from me, from beyond me; I floated above us and watched him tease me, wished I was corporeal so I could smack him on the back of his head. Finally he pulled my underwear down and threw it on the floor. He fucked me with his tongue and lips and fingers until I gushed again and again and again, all over him and his bed and his sheets.

I had to fuck this man, whose last name I didn't know, whose past I didn't care about or his future or his dreams, his childhood pets or religious beliefs; I had to have him in me and it had to be now.

He knelt above me, stroking his cock and staring at me as I shivered. I held my arms out to him; my hair was all over the pillows; I probably looked like a drowning maiden in the sea of his sheets.

"Condom?" I whispered.

He nodded, smiled small, and reached over to his nightstand to rummage around for a silver square.

He rolled it onto his cock looking at me with one eyebrow raised, while I lay back on the pillows and idly fingered myself. He kissed me, pinched my nipples hard, went down for a few good licks before coming back up to my face and kissing me, his mouth smelling like my come, rubbing his cock against my clit. I bit his lower lip, not softly, and he finally relented and slipped inside of me inch by inch.

We both inhaled shakily, like car accident victims walking with canes on ice.

His penis felt like a true extension of himself; not just something he was wildly thrusting, hoping to hit something good, but a deliberate appendage he controlled as easily and naturally as his hand. He pushed inside of me, gently and persistently, knocking my cervix as surely as he'd ring a doorbell, and I gasped. It felt good but hurt, and I couldn't decide if I wanted to push back or whimper.

"Am I hurting you?"

"Yeah, but...don't worry about it. Just keep going."

"Why shouldn't I worry about hurting you?"

I didn't have an answer for that.

So I did both. I flexed around him, and he gasped back. We had found our back-and-forth rhythm and were gaining speed when he stopped suddenly and pulled me up with him so we were sitting face-to-face. He hadn't even withdrawn from me; he raised me as easily as a rag doll and I let him. I wanted him to flop me around like an ancient Raggedy Ann doll.

I kissed him long and deep, fucking his mouth with my tongue, trying to get it as deep inside him as he was inside of me. His cock jumped inside me.

"I'm not moving until you come again," he said.

"Is this a challenge or a threat? A bet or a promise?"

"All of it, all of it," he said and kissed me with those wide, rough lips. I ran my nails up his sides, circled his nipples, lingeringly pinched one and then the other. He bit his lip.

"You are making this very, very difficult."

"What are we betting, exactly?"

"It's a bet we both win," he said and began slowly rubbing my clit, up and down, a deliberate stroke that I could feel lift my clit so it hovered, tip in the air, until he released it and started again. Up and down, with him jumping deep inside me, so deep I imagined him nudging my ovaries and rearranging my guts. I flexed around his cock, hard, dancingly, over and over and over again until I came so hard I couldn't see for a few seconds. His beautiful dotted shoulders had red fingernail-shaped crescents beginning to swell among those clouds, tiny suns to remember me by.

He put his arms behind me and gently laid me back down on the bed. There was no longer a need for speed or gentleness, no doorbell ringing or questionable knocking; just sheer, brutal fucking. His clouds and flowers would be destroyed, but that's why artists do touch-ups, right? Sweat dripped down his cheeks and neck and onto my chest; I licked his chin. His eyes were open; he stared into me and past me, and it scared me a little, how almost angry and sad he seemed. Sometimes people cry when they come; it's happened to me. Never to a guy I was with, though.

He kissed me, sloppy and wet and panting, moaning into my

mouth, still staring at me and into me and past me, still scaring me. He thrust a few last times and I felt his cock thrum with orgasm. He fell onto my chest and kissed my shoulder, and I felt something wet drip down from my shoulder to my chest and lie between my breasts.

I couldn't tell if it was sweat or tears.

PICTURES OF LILLY

Chrissie Bentley

It is said that a stereotype is only truly offensive (and stereo-typical) if it is true. In that case, my memories of a certain Adults Only theater, in a medium-sized East Coast city in the mid-1970s are very offensive indeed.

Even from the outside, the building stood out like a dirty nail on a manicured hand, an off-white pile that was erected in the '30s as the latest in contemporary architecture, and had neither been painted nor refurbished since then. Once it had indeed been a proud and beautiful theater, but the mainstream movies had long stopped playing there.

Instead, a proprietor who looked as seedy as his establish-ment specialized in what the low-key marquee insisted were Continental and Scandinavian features, all of which apparently starred the same blowsily made-up cartoon blonde, scantily clad and long since defaced beneath precisely the kind of graffiti you'd expect to find in such a place—ink-scrawled cocks and balls that assailed her from every direction, ribald commentaries that blossomed in speech bubbles, and enough jets of Magic Markered semen to float a battleship.

The place never closed. Early morning, on the way to class; late into the evening, on the way home from a friend's house and at any hour in between, one of two or three bored-looking youths would be seated in the ticket booth; and, occasionally, you'd see an actual customer shuffling in or out of the main door, and he'd be as clichéd as the establishment itself. He really would look furtive, he really would be wearing a raincoat, and nine times out of ten, he really would be wearing a flat cap, which he'd pull down over his eyes the moment he saw someone else on the street outside.

But there was one aspect of the experience that was not a stereotype; that was, in fact, so bizarre that even those of us who were aware of it were scarcely able to voice it out loud, for fear that the very act of open discussion might end the magic there and then. Every Thursday afternoon (but only Thursday afternoons), sometime before we turned out of class, the emergency exit at the back of the building would be mysteriously unbolted and would remain that way all evening.

The first few weeks after we discovered this presumably magical portal, the four of us simply stood by the opening, squinting into the darkness on the other side, listening to the soundtrack that crackled off the screen: groans, gasps, cries and crescendos, all set to a kind of pulsing neo-rock music, played exclusively, it seemed through a wah-wah pedal.

Occasionally a snatch of dialogue would emerge amid the grunting; occasionally, the actual meaning of the words might be comprehended by one or other of us, but even if they weren't, the sentence itself would soak into our collective psyche, to become a sort of in-joke secret weapon, to be deployed whenever the adult world grew too demanding.

"Did you finish your history assignment?" "Go lick it off your tits." And I often wonder whether I was the only one of us who experienced a secret frisson of excitement at the very thought of doing just that...of raising one breast and lowering my head and then running my tongue through the thick pool of come that a lover had just deposited there. I don't know, maybe I was. But when one of our number—I think it was Wanda—suggested that we actually pass through the door and watch instead of merely listening to the movies, I was the first to agree.

We were no strangers to "bunking" into the movies for free. Every movie-house in town had its weak point, be it a back door, a bathroom window or simply a turn-a-blind-eye manager, through which a stealthy form could slip and thrill to those quaintly X-rated flicks that no one at that time would ever have dreamed an impressionable teen should witness: *Straw Dogs, Soldier Blue, The Night Porter, The Exorcist.* If the marquee mandated twenty-one-and over, we were in there, and it was astonishing just how discriminating we became, able within ten minutes or so of knowing whether the movie was worth watching (bush, blood, tits and terror), or if we should up and march out and do something interesting instead.

This experience was different, though. You went in through the out door, down a smokily unlit passageway and into an auditorium that was scarcely the size of a classroom, with a screen no bigger than a bedsheet. The room seemed darker than the usual theater and the audience more restless. There were rustling sounds, mostly, interspersed with heavy breathing. "Someone," Lisa whispered in my ear, "is having a quiet jerk-off."

Only it wasn't so quiet. And it wasn't just someone. Judging from the rustling sounds, half the men in the room were at it.

A movie was already playing, a scratchy-looking black-and-white opus, whose plot—so far as we could distinguish one—

was, how far could a cock slide up a fat woman's asshole before it bumped tips with the other one, which was sliding down her throat? And that, we quickly learned, was one of the more erudite efforts. But to four girls who had only ever seen sex in a Hollywood production, where it's camera work and angles that give the scene its sensation, even the crudest coupling was fascinating stuff.

By the time they hit their late teens, most girls are at least theoretically aware of the mechanics of sex. They know where "it" is meant to go, they've heard of the other places it can go, and they've already thought of one or two more where they'd like to think it could go. Even in an age in which Internet Porn, Prime Time Smut, and Cable Specials weren't simply unheard of, they weren't even dreamed up, popular culture had already built sufficient hints and clues into its makeup to enable a well-developed imagination to join up most of the dots. And if there's one thing about a teenaged girl that is well developed, it's her imagination.

What was taking place on that screen, however, went beyond anything we had ever thought up. The titles of the movies themselves are long forgotten; so, in terms of actual happenstance, are most of the "plots." But the impression they left, the wonder they aroused, the excitement they provoked and the sheer sense of injustice that they left behind—why doesn't that ever happen to me?—would remain long after we left the building that evening, through the never-ending week that followed and probably well into adulthood as well.

Had I ever seen a hard cock before? Never. Had I ever watched a guy come? Never. Staring at the screen that first afternoon, I realized that everything...every single thing that I had ever read, heard, seen or been told about sex wasn't simply wrong, it was ridiculous.

There was no "romance" here, no hand-holding, no eyes meeting across a darkened room while electricity flashed between their souls. It was hunger, it was greed, it was naked animal passion. It was cocks and cunts and juices and jizz. Love didn't even enter into it.

And it was quick. Of course the main movie was "full length"; an hour, maybe even ninety minutes, and there'd be plot and dialogue around the frenzied fucking. For me, though, the real meat was the supporting program, anything up to two hours' worth of shorts that could have been shot at any time since my granny was a girl, which made no attempt whatsoever at being anything other than pure sexuality.

They were rarely longer than nine or ten minutes. "That's because ten minutes is the length of the average jerk-off," disclosed Wanda, whose knowledge of such things was rarely questioned (alone among us, she had an older brother, you see). But they didn't need to be any longer than that, because there was more "action" crammed into one ten-minute dirty than you'd catch in a lifetime of watching Hollywood blockbusters.

I remembered reading a review of *Last Tango In Paris* that said how realistic the sex scenes were meant to be, and when I saw it, I agreed. They were realistic. But realistic isn't real, and no amount of fancy lighting will ever be a substitute for a close-up of a hard, thick dick slamming into a gaping, wet pussy. So why even bother faking it?

The most amazing thing of all, though; the one question that has remained with me longer than almost any other puzzle from my past—how was it that four barely legal teenaged virgins, all giggles and curls and noticeable curves, could sit week-in, week-out, in a darkened room full of masturbating men and not get hit on even once?

It's not as though nobody knew we were there. In fact, on

more than one occasion, guys actually got up and moved to another seat when they saw us trooping down the aisle. Maybe they were worried that we'd put them off their stroke? Masturbation is a solitary occupation, after all. Occasionally you'd catch a surreptitious glance out of the corner of your eye, and you'd find yourself wondering what the guy was thinking. Was he looking at your tits while he was beating his meat? But that was it.

Except once. One afternoon, the action crept off the screen, slipped down the aisle past a dozen or so rows and began playing out so close to me that I could have reached out and touched it. And I might have, as well. Except Wendy got in before me, and she wasn't the sort of girl who shared. I think she was an only child.

I remember the movie like it was yesterday: *The Sexorcist,* a blatant attempt to cling to the coattails of the post-*Exorcist* boom in supernatural chillers, shot through with a series of extraordinarily explicit sexual encounters, most of them led by the delectable Lilly Lamarr.

What ever happened to Lilly? I never once spotted her in any other movie...maybe she burned out making this one. It was pretty heavy going, after all, and her character comes to a very grisly end. But still she remains my all-time cinematic heroine, the one girl with whom, as I sat watching the movie, I would have traded places in a flash. And why? Because when she sucked dick, I saw my every dream and fantasy come true.

The problem with *Deep Throat,* I always thought, was that no matter how into it Linda Lovelace seems to be, the fact is, she really doesn't look good while she's doing it. Her face is all screwed up; there are veins and tendons sticking out. She's not sucking the cock in, she's vomiting it out. It's just not attractive, and any guy on the receiving end of that is going to be thinking,

Well, it feels great, but does she have to pull those faces?

There's a visual aesthetic to blow jobs that goes beyond the actual act, and most guys will tell you, a girl who relaxes into the experience and looks like she's having the time of her life, is a lot more exciting than one who's straining and spluttering and looks like she's coughing up a hair ball. Lamarr fulfills those criteria and then keeps on going.

She's an artist, an expert, the Bolshoi of blow jobs, and when her man comes, she opens her mouth just wide enough for all the juice to come dribbling out, simply so she can have the fun of sucking it all back in again. And again and again. I was watching her relish every inch of those dicks, and you can forget wet panties. I was soaking into the seat itself...and wouldn't that be a treat for the next guy to sit there? "This movie's so hot I can smell it!"

Anyway, I'm sitting there, literally flooding myself, when someone sat down just two seats away from me. I didn't pay any attention at first, but every so often, a movement would flutter in the corner of my eye. It wasn't fast, and it certainly wasn't furtive; at first I thought he was simply munching popcorn. But then Wendy, sitting on my other side, nudged me. "Are you watching this guy?"

I looked. He had his cock out...and that was unusual; most of the guys we'd seen playing with themselves had their hands wedged down the front of their trousers or maybe covered their laps with a coat. But not this one. Bold as you like, it was out in the open, quivering hard and pointing bolt upright, and he was stroking it, a long, slow sweep with one hand and then, as he reached the tip, and his fingers hung there, the other hand would start at the bottom. And between each sweep, his free hand would go up to his face, and he'd sniff his own fingers and palm.

I glanced at the screen. The movie was into one of its plot interludes. I turned back to the guy. His eyes were glued to the screen, but his hands were still working their magic, slow and patient.

Wendy nudged me again. "How old do you reckon he is?"

"I dunno. Midtwenties, maybe?"

"He's cute."

"He's all right."

"Watch this." Wendy rose, placed her purse on her seat and squeezed past our friends on her other side. She walked a smart circuit around the theater, and then headed back to her seat from the other end of the row...the end where the guy was sitting. She'd have to get past him to regain her own seat.

All three of us were watching her now. Laughing, we'd often wondered what would happen if we crept up on one of the guys sitting around us and placed one hand where his was, just to see what it felt like. I never thought Wendy would be the one who actually did it, though. Looked like Lilly Lamarr was working her magic on her as well.

She'd reached him. By the light of the movie, I could see her mouth "Excuse me," and the guy's look of absolute shock as he registered her standing there. He made to stand up to let her pass, while frantically trying to tuck his cock out of sight, but as Wendy passed him, her own hand gripped it.

Have you ever startled a kitten when it's doing something it shouldn't be? That's what his face looked like, frozen, wide-eyed, bewildered...and those eyes grew wider still, as Wendy settled down into the empty seat between him and me, still clutching that twitching erection. Then she leaned forward a little.

With her nose just millimeters away from his cock, she took a deep breath, then clasped one of his wrists with her free hand, sniffed at that, too, and slowly licked her tongue up his palm.

The guy had shifted his feet a little; he was standing in front of her now (I hoped nobody behind them was trying to watch the screen!), and I could see everything around Wendy's fingers: the thick vein that ran up the side of the shaft, the thick mushroom head, the forest of dark hair at the base.

There was a kind of bend in his dick. Although the guy was facing Wendy, the eyelet in his helmet was pointing straight at me. I took a breath, hoping I could catch his scent, but my own was so powerful that I'd need to get a lot closer before that happened. Close enough to smell him, close enough to taste...

Wendy read my mind, moving forward herself. Maneuvering myself in my seat, I saw her tongue snake out at the underside of his helmet, and I heard his gasp as she made contact. She'd been eating mints all the time we'd been in the movie house; would their tingle translate itself to her tongue? Or did that even matter now? What did it feel like to have such a sensitive part of your body immersed in the warmth of someone else's mouth, to feel the heat of their spit soaking into the nerve-ends? I glanced up at his face, which held an expression of absolute pleasure that ironed out every line in his forehead, as her mouth inched itself languorously over the bulb.

A moment of irrational, unreasonable envy swept over me—partly because of what she was doing (and the knowledge that, had I only thought of it first, that could have been me sitting where she was), but also because...she looked like she knew what she was doing. Had she done this before? Who with? When? I seethed at the sight of the experience she seemed to be exerting here, the calm and casual manner with which she held the head of that hard-on in her mouth, before slowly withdrawing...not quite all the way, he was balanced on her lips now...and then taking it in again, a little deeper, a little harder.

Now she was sucking. I could see her cheeks working, her

tongue, too. It looked incredible. I thought, with all the movies we'd watched, that I knew everything there was to know about giving good head. But watching it actually unfold in the flesh alongside me, that was a completely different experience. I could hear Wendy's lips slurping at his hard flesh; could hear his breathing accelerate, from light gasps to groaning pants. Was he coming?

I threw a glance at the screen. Lilly was at it as well, sucking on the devil's dick, drawing him deep into her mouth. "Bite it, hurt it, bite it," he was muttering, and the camera closed in as her teeth sank hard into his helmet. Christ, I wanted some of that. I could see the actress's saliva flowing, thick and clear, flooding to celebrate the taste of a man. Her teeth looked sharp; that must have hurt. But was it a bad pain or a good one? It had to be good—how could anything that looks that wonderful feel like anything else?

I turned back to Wendy, hoping she'd tire, or lose interest or something, anything, so that I could pounce and suck and bite and taste. But no, she was moving faster now, graceful swoops down his slick prick; I could see her lips straining to enfold more of his length in her mouth—he must have been halfway in, how much more could she take? And, more importantly, how much more could he take?

He was loud now, his groans competing with the on-screen demon's, and when the actor came, with a cry of exquisite release, so did the guy. I saw Wendy's head jerk back with shock, as his come shot out, showering her shoulder, spattering her face. If I'd been quicker, I could have thrown myself into the line of fire, felt it slap against my skin and then licked it away again. Instead, I felt like grabbing Wendy and shaking her. *You wasted it!* I wanted to say. *Has Lilly taught you nothing?*

But I was fascinated as well, watching as the cock began almost instantly to subside, the last thick drops of white collecting at the tip to drip reluctantly to the floor. Their owner, too, was limp, leaning back on the seats behind him, collecting his breath, gathering his wits and gazing at Wendy with such undying devotion that, as she stood up and squeezed past me, wordlessly returning to her own seat, I thought he was going to cry.

Instead he just stood there for a few moments more, slowly comprehending the fact that it was over, that Wendy wasn't even going to look at him again, let alone speak. Then he buttoned himself up and walked away.

We sat in silence for a moment. Then Wanda spoke.

"So what was that all about?"

Wendy didn't answer immediately. "I felt like it. We've done so much talking, I just wanted to see what it was really like."

So it was her first time. I felt a pang of relief.

Wanda again. "What does it taste like?"

Again, Wendy was silent, weighing her words before she committed to them. "Salty. Like a pretzel. A glazed pretzel. It was okay."

"Just okay?" That was Lisa.

"It was fun. It would've been better if I'd been more comfortable, and my jaw did start to hurt after a bit. And he kept trying to push too far. But yeah, it's okay."

"What about at the end?" I asked. "How did you know it was...he was...coming?"

"I didn't, he just jerked away and it startled me. But I'm glad he did, I think. I caught a bit in my mouth, and..." She made a face. "Salty old socks. You probably need to get used to it."

I looked up at the screen. Lilly didn't seem to mind it so much, and just watching the expression on her face, as her umpteenth mouthful dribbled down a dick, I knew that, when my time finally came, I was going to love it as well, no matter

how much getting used to it took. And, unlike a lot of the res‌
lutions I've made over the years (to quit smoking, get plenty of
exercise, never pet strange dogs…), I'm proud to say that's the
one I've stuck to.

The Sexorcist was one of the last movies we ever saw at that
shabby old movie house with the mysteriously unlocked door;
one of the last truly great ones, anyway. Other people learned the
secret, including some who might otherwise have paid for their
membership; and others, who didn't believe that such estab-
lishments had any right to exist in the first place. One balmy
Thursday the following spring, we arrived at the back door
at the same time as always to find two uniformed policemen
standing in the shadows within.

We ran; they stayed, and the next time we passed by, the
building was empty, the doors were chained, the marquee had
been stripped bare. Only the cartoon blonde remained, and even
she'd had a billposter slapped over her mouth. Even at our age,
that seemed strangely symbolic.

Alyssa Turner

I rarely have the time to treat myself to anything. Call me a workaholic, but starting a PR firm from the ground up has left my days jam-packed with serving the requirements of others. Demanding as they are, I have to be grateful that my list of clients is rapidly growing, and it's looking like my business will actually turn a profit some day. Still, to keep my sanity I say my daily affirmation: *it will all be worth it when I can hire someone else to put up with all the bullshit,* and then I get my ass on another plane to work my magic on some new product launch or fundraising breakfast. All that back and forth can be murder on your body; not enough sleep, too much time in coach...not enough sex. By the time I'm ready to return, I'm guaranteed to be stressed out, mentally spent and in desperate need of a massage. After one particularly long and aggravating day on the road, I decided that some relaxation at the hands of another was just what I deserved.

I stopped at the concierge desk. "Your website mentioned

that you have a spa," I inquired of a vapid-looking young woman, interrupting her not-so-discreet conversation with one of the porters about her last booty call. She glanced my way, clearly inconvenienced by my pesky desire to be helped. "I'd like a massage. Can I make an appointment here?" I asked her directly.

She sighed and told the guy she would give him the rest of the details later. I wondered if that tactic would be successful for her; dangling the fruit on the tree to show off how ripe it is. From the look on his face, I'd have said that it was working. "Do you want a male or female therapist?" she asked finally, staring at the computer screen.

"I'll take whoever is available first. I know it's short notice, but I was hoping to get a back rub in about an hour." I tried to make a joke: "You know, it's like an emergency." It went completely over her head, and she tapped at the keyboard, sucking her teeth in annoyance. "If it's not too much trouble," I added sarcastically, becoming annoyed a bit myself—confounded that a four-star hotel could have such a two-star employee working for them.

"It's not a problem—it's just this dumb computer. It froze on me again. I'll have to reboot it." She tapped impatiently on the enter key a few more times in exasperation. "Just tell me what room you're in; I'll send someone up."

"Up?" I asked, with confusion.

"Yes, up to your room. The spa closes at six during the week." She finally gave me some eye contact. "It will cost you thirty-five dollars more an hour for in-room service; you okay with that?"

She was really pissing me off with her fucked-up attitude, but not having to leave my room again for the night sounded great. Hell, yes, I wanted to pay the extra thirty-five dollars. "What time can I expect someone?" I asked simply.

"Soon," she answered, with no promises for specifics.

Luckily, room service was more responsive, and in a half hour I was sequestered in my temporary hideout with a grilled-chicken salad and a glass of wine, eager for my pamper session to begin.

Around eight there was a knock on my door. Already showered and nude under my fluffy white hotel robe, I checked to confirm that my masseur had arrived. When I opened the door, I suddenly realized that I certainly did care whether I had a male or female therapist. In fact, I couldn't have asked for someone more perfect for my needs that evening. He was delicious looking with longish sand-colored hair and a cleft in his chin that was only a bit deeper than the dimples advertised in his warm, pleasant smile. Suspended effortlessly in one hand was a folded massage table; in the other, a large bag with towels spilling over the top. I stood there a moment, drinking him in. *That idiot at the concierge desk actually got something right,* I thought and returned the friendly smile with a raised eyebrow.

"I'm Sean," he said. "Have a seat; it will just take me a moment to set up." I sat in the middle of the bed watching him keenly, examining his fluid motions as he went about unpacking his equipment. He seemed to notice that he had my undivided attention and made sure to meet my eyes with a wink. "You look like you could use a little TLC," he said securing the legs of his table. "Long day?"

"Long enough," I replied coolly, pondering whether this was something he said to break the ice with all of his clients. He tilted his head and let his gaze travel into the shadows of my open collar. If he weren't so beautiful, I'd have instinctively pulled it tighter around my neck. Instead I found myself biting my lip in consideration of his angled jaw and amber-colored eyes and stretching backward onto my elbows, certain that my robe would fall slightly off my shoulder. Just as he was finishing setting up there was another knock on the door. Assuming that room service was retrieving my tray, I answered with it already in hand.

The rather muscular guy standing in my doorway was just as hot as the one already in my room, but a bit darker—both in hue and in spirit. He stood there with his cherry red lips offsetting his white teeth, grinning ruefully. "Hi there, are you ready for your massage?" he asked in a smoky tone. As I took note of his identical spa-issued white shirt and pants, he spotted his colleague prepped to begin an overhaul of my tired body. Entering my room, he said with a frown, "What are you doing here, Sean? This is my call."

"I don't think so, Mike, you'd better check with the desk."

"I have the room number right here." Mike moved closer to him with an official-looking piece of paper in his hand. Continuing under his breath he muttered, "This gig is mine and so is the tip that comes with it," and he nodded in my direction.

"I have the same work order, so I guess we'll have to go with who got here first." Sean was holding his ground and made no moves to disassemble his table.

I held my up hands, interrupting them with my tendency to take control of a situation. "Why don't you both stay and split the time that I've paid for; if you do a good job, then you can split the tip." *No need to let either of you go to waste,* I added silently, pressing my lips together in anticipation of their response. I figured I might as well find a way to take advantage of the mistake and enjoy both of them for the price of one. They nodded and seemed to think it was a fair solution, so I peeked into my purse to see how much cash I had.

Unfortunately there was only a crisp fifty dollar bill. "You'll have to break it," I told them apologetically, waving it in the air.

It was Mike who came up with an alternative. "Maybe we could let you decide who deserves it more," he said and glanced at Sean. "We'll each take turns working out your kinks, like you said, and the one who does the best job wins."

I had to admit, the notion of two ridiculously hot guys rubbing their hands over my body in a competition for my approval made me cream a little. I played the moment out, tapping my finger on my bottom lip and looking each of them up and down before responding. "Let's find out which one of you has the magic touch," I said finally, and after they turned for my privacy, I disrobed to let the games begin.

Facedown, I settled on the table, while Sean placed a towel over my bare bottom and Mike arranged my hair to expose my neck. Simultaneously their fingers danced lightly over my skin, giving me goose bumps even while performing these common tasks. Cool oil dripped over my back, and the first set of hands took hold of me from above, kneading each of my shoulders. I melted into the table as Sean worked through the pent-up tension there. Instantly, I felt the residue of my delayed flight, my missed meeting and the unsavory comments from my disappointed client fall away among his circular impressions in my flesh. His touch was definitive, yet not overly firm, and I wondered if he intended to be turning me on with his warm breath softly beating on the back of my neck.

When I was completely loose, his fingers slipped down the edges of my shoulder blades and briefly grazed the sides of my breasts. My skin lit with sensation as his hands continued down my torso and under the towel concealing my rear end. This endless stroke proceeded in one long motion to reach my inner thighs. Once there, he softly caressed the supple flesh, before gently spreading my legs apart. Cool air swept past the silky wetness developing in my most tender spot.

"How are you enjoying it so far?" he asked, his two fingers experiencing the slickness firsthand as they swept casually over my soft folds. I had to wonder if it was an accident. Either way, my hips rose off the table to find his hand again. It was reflexive—a subconscious response to the bliss he was granting me with his talented fingers.

My reaction wasn't overlooked. His fingers swept back over my ass and to my waist, then down again under the towel and in between my legs, where this time they lingered in the elixir gathering there. "Is this the spot that has been giving you the most trouble?" he ventured boldly, and I asked myself the same question. I had been working like a dog for the past year and could count on one hand the occasions I'd found the time to invest in my sex life. Career minded to a fault, my drive for success had left me impatient with small talk and bored with first dates, let alone second ones. Worse still, I hadn't even made a single fuck-buddy since my last boyfriend. This thought caused me to think about the dumb chick at the concierge desk and her obvious advantage over me in that category. I realized that most of my tension was right in my underworked vagina. It was high time that I let someone help with that, and he seemed perfectly up for the task, not to mention his hunky colleague waiting patiently on the bed. I decided to answer Sean with a long sighing moan while he slowly dipped his two fingers inside of me, and then retracted them with expert precision.

A smile tickled the corners of my mouth, and I openly let my hips play puppet with his fingers, like a marionette on sticky strings stretching from my cunt. In and out he sent them slowly, and my entire body began to gyrate with his controlled timing, my moans increasing in frequency. He leaned forward, his shirt tickling my back as he placed his mouth only inches from my ear. Sean's words were heavy in his throat, moving over his lips as smoothly as his fingers entered my wetness. "Ah, yes. That's the spot...isn't it?"

It was really not a question, and I left no room for misinterpretation as I purred a syrupy, "Yes." His lips did not leave my ear and his breathing, hard and smoldering, spoke of his own enjoyment.

Curious to see how my other masseur was reacting to this scene, I lifted my head to find Mike rubbing his rather large bulge through his white cotton pants. Meeting my gaze he boasted, "Just get ready for what I will do for you next," and I thought he looked too good for words.

I was enticed. "Why don't you show me what you have in mind?"

He needed no further encouragement, and in an instant he was in position at my side. Sean's fingers, which had pleasured me so effectively, retracted one last time, and Mike instructed me to turn over. Holding a towel up for privacy in the traditional fashion, he allowed me a moment to arrange myself comfortably, face up. When he placed the folded towel over the very zones I was hoping to have attended to, I wondered what he could possibly have in mind to surpass Sean's performance.

Once I was settled, Mike asked quite plainly, "Where is your vibrator?" His mouth curled slightly in a teasing smirk, and he blinked in a leisurely way, confident of his presumption.

I crinkled my brow, hating to be read so perfectly but thinking his cockiness was sexy as hell. Indeed, his instincts were correct—I am seldom without my favorite toy for any extended time. "It's in the night table," I confessed, and he retrieved it with a bit of a swagger. As he slid the humming staff under the folded towel, I considered how erotic it was to be so modestly concealed while he shamelessly fondled me with it.

Though I made no secret of my eagerness to experience the tricks he had planned, he only gently tapped my vibrator on the surface playfully, making me squirm and whimper for more. I cooed at its touch and fought the urge to open my legs for him, challenging myself to maintain the same amount of composure that he exhibited with his calculated maneuvers. My eyes, which had been closed, refocused to find him staring at me, intently studying my expressions and recognizing every occasion when he discovered a sweet spot. Finally, when I could wait no more, he moved it inside, while his index finger began to rub my clit. Both hands performed their tasks with remarkable skill. His eyes were locked with mine as he smiled back at my beaming grin. I gripped the sheet on the table, lying there, enjoying every stroke. He had a gentle and subdued technique, with a slow and desirous rhythm that left me consumed with lust. I cried out for more and he upped the pace and vibration, his finger continuing to sweep against my swollen bud. Nearing the point of no return, I felt that familiar tingling pressure build, and I was sure that I would erupt any minute.

My teeth clenched behind pursed lips, and Mike, who was completely in tune to the flood that was nearing, whispered, "That's it, come all over my hand," while squeezing his fingers into my thigh. I pulled the towel away to give him a better look, allowing him to delight in his accomplishment. He took full advantage of the view, and his mouth fell open, tasting the air between us.

Sean, who had maintained his position at my side, was enjoying the spectacle just as much. He crouched next to me, skimming the surface of my torso with the palm of his hand.

"You are so incredibly sexy," he said and placed his fingers into my parted lips, reminding me of where they had been. Then he added with a nibble on my ear, "I don't even care about the stupid competition. I just want more of you."

I answered both of them with a throat-rasping, "Yessss," and I turned to kiss Sean, shuddering, still in orgasm. It was the sweetest release I'd had in long time, so selfishly received for my enjoyment alone. Sean lifted me off the table and carried me to the bed. I waved for Mike to join us and grabbed him by the collar. "I think we would all like some more," I breathed, and he nodded in agreement, taking his first taste of me from my collarbone. Sean promptly followed, licking my breast and suckling softly on my nipple. I arched my back and stretched myself long against the plush down comforter beneath me, reveling in their wet mouths as they trailed over my skin.

Sean slurped on my hip bone and Mike grazed his teeth against my jaw, teasing me and driving me wild. Next he solicited my tongue to dance lightly with his, and Sean slipped his lips onto my sopping vagina. The room was spinning, as I lost myself in the heart-pounding whirlwind of pure ecstasy. Sean kissed at my pussy carefully at first, tasting me, savoring me. And when he plunged his undulating tongue into my silky cavern, I moaned into Mike's open mouth. Our delicate kiss ignited, while Sean bathed my clit with saliva and sipped on my juices until the rush of satisfaction began to fill me once again. I tore my lips away from Mike only to cry out, "Don't stop!" But Sean did stop nonetheless, rising to his feet and speaking with glistened lips.

"More?" he asked, with the marked weight of one simple word.

"Yes," I uttered, breathless with want. He was unzipping his pants immediately and releasing his ready cock. I threw my legs apart. "More," I confirmed again, propping up on my elbows to watch as he placed his throbbing head at my entry. While he pushed into me, Mike lavished my tongue once again with his own. He filled his hands with my breasts, and Sean's fingers wrapped around my hips, steadying them as I bucked violently against him. It was only moments before I careened into another orgasm, this one rigorous and unabashed. I screamed, loud enough to startle myself, surprised that I could come that hard. He withdrew, stroking himself to his own final release and falling over with a hard sigh next to me.

It would be an hour before we would pick up round two and I would have the pleasure of seeing Mike's beautifully formed and remarkable-sized cock. Revitalized and ready to know what further pleasures awaited me, I pulled it from his white cotton pants and watched it spring forward, ready to show and prove its promise. Sean sat up in the bed, roused by our shifting, and leaned against the headboard. I placed myself between his legs, resting my back against his hairless chest.

Mike approached from the front, kneeling in front of me. We communicated without words—through only the intensity of our piercing stares—while Sean caressed my thighs with the cadence of a butterfly, sparking my nerve endings anew. Then with a nuzzle to my temple, he lifted my legs in his open palms to spread me wide for Mike. The look on Mike's face signaled that I was in store for a wild ride, and I braced myself against Sean, holding on to his neck with my raised arms. Mike slid into me with total knowledge of his daunting size, allowing me to become accustomed to the feel of him filling me. I sucked in a slow, deep breath as he pressed deeper, while thoughts of Sean's cock throbbing against my back lapped delightfully at my subconscious. Sean lifted my legs higher, rotating my hips upward while Mike grabbed my ankles and gently spread my legs even farther apart. Then he licked his luscious lips and proceeded to withdraw from me all the way. I gasped, and he smirked knowing just what a game he was playing. He positioned himself at my portal a second time, and I arched against Sean, reaching for Mike's missing cock with my dripping cunt. With one deep stroke he filled me again and then withdrew entirely.

Desperate for it now I yelled, "Fuck me, you tease!" And he grinned, as full of himself as ever, though rightfully so—in that moment he was holding all the cards. Sadistically, he would subject me to one more slow and agonizingly sweet introduction of his rigid penis before he finally gave me what I wanted, whipping his cock in and out with abandon and ushering us both to yet another fiery explosion.

Breathless, I relaxed my trembling frame onto Sean, my body a mound of tingling nerves and electric chills. I could feel the faint meanderings of Sean's fingers as he ran them absently through my hair and the warm weight of Mike's head on my thigh as he used it for a pillow. We stayed like that for some time, drifting in and out of sleep and replaying the night's events in our thoughts and dreams. Our final good-byes during the wee hours of the morning would find us all in agreement about two things: the race for my fifty bucks had gone right out the window somewhere after my second orgasm, and we should definitely get together again if I happened to return to town. But at that moment, lying there nestled between the two of them and floating on a level of satisfaction I hadn't imagined I would find during any massage session—I silently called it a tie.

I, ANITA

Lana Fox

The Baron first set eyes on me during my burlesque, in which I slow-danced in a corset with a garter belt and stockings. I enjoyed swinging my hips within the tight, boned basque, its sleek red silk stretched taut. Apart from my costume, I had only a wooden chair, which awaited my arrival on the limelit stage. Leaning forward, I'd raise my knee and place my heeled sandal upon the seat, smoothing a stocking along my thigh, my red lips pouting, my eyes heavily kohled. I used my body, arching my spine so my breasts pushed up against the strapless bodice, as if at any moment, in their buoyancy, they'd spring from the fabric. There, as the music played, I'd slowly gyrate, making love to the men with my stare. Not that I could see them—they were lost in the shadows—but I could feel their desire burning my flesh, could hear their throaty cries.

But this was just the prelude; I was famous for the wooden chair. A member of the audience would be led to the stage where I'd take his hand, and his dewy vulnerability never failed to affect me. As he sat in the chair, I knelt at his feet clutching his knees, fingers covered with rings and bangles—before I unbuttoned his flies.

There with quiet moans rising from our audience, I'd take the man's sex in my hands and with my tongue, my mouth, my slick-glossed lips, I would bestow my pleasure. Velvet Tongue, they called me, for that's how I worked: with my breasts rising inside my corset, and the garter-straps digging into my thighs, and my dark curls tumbling, I'd lick and suck, rub and tease, my own sex growing wetter, until I'd feel him clutching at his seat with trembling, white knuckles.

I'd somehow know exactly what each man craved the most.

He'd yell out, bucking into my mouth, crying wildly as he filled my throat—thrusting over and over, he'd often fill me so fully that the fluid would seep from the corners of my mouth. At other times, when he reached the point of no return, I'd know to pull back, allowing the first flash of my oil-rubbed breasts to catch his coming. The pale stream would streak across my cleavage and down the boned bodice; the moans of approval from the audience made me long to touch myself. The man would gratefully collapse. Whoever he was, he'd ask me out on a date.

I always told them no.

Until I met the Baron.

Whenever I returned backstage, I'd lock the door to my dressing room, and there on the chair I'd brought from my act, I would slide two fingers inside my slick lace and rub myself quickly, the fluid still warm on my nipples, arching as I came. Thus, before I met the Baron, I never had to be close to a man. Sex for me was either public or terribly alone.

I didn't know how miserable I was.

Well, you will hear dastardly things said of the Baron, and

most of them are true. How he held sleeping girls in his bed and touched himself without their knowing; how he fucked his wives then left them, robbing them of their money, counting on the fact that they'd be too high from his loving to report his hasty crimes. Though the rank of baron is the lowest of the nobles, he still had money and the manners of a lord—could hide his true nature beneath a decorous mask. But as with all rogues, he was also a liberator.

I, you see, was a little like the Baron.

The night he arrived, it was raining outside. I'd just returned from the stage, the chair in my arms, and I entered my dressing room to find him standing at the window smoking a clove cigarette, elegantly slouched to one side. He was wearing a red velvet jacket, which matched my corset, and his black hair glinted in the light from old-style lamp I'd set on my dressing table. He turned, his face lascivious, as if he knew all my ills, and I noticed his tiny moustache like that of a classic villain.

I asked what he was doing there.

He told me to put down the chair.

I challenged him: "Why?"

He said, "I'll take you over my knee."

I threw back my head and laughed, but no sooner had I done so than he was grabbing the chair and throwing it down on the boards. He kicked the door shut behind us, clasped me by the arm, sat in the chair and pulled me across his lap. I gasped out, astonished, before I felt him spanking me, each strike making a slapping noise against my lace-clasped buttocks. I could smell his cologne rising from his flesh. Aroused as I was from the man I'd just pleasured onstage, each spank made me more wanting and hot. I parted my thighs a little, hoping he'd touch my sex, but he kept to my buttocks, talking as he struck: "You are talented, Anita. But you must learn to relent. You won't achieve true heights unless you accept your nature." His spanking grew fiercer, tugging at the lace of my knickers—the rough material plucked at the lips of my pussy and I begged him for more.

It was true I had always kept up my guard. As a girl, I'd been so quiet, giving nothing I couldn't control. Even my secrets weren't quite true—when you lie you're rarely vulnerable. I was raised by my uncle, who once called me a woman of wax. There was a distance in his eyes as he said it, and we were eating rabbit stew. "But no," he said, "wax melts." I reminded him that he'd never once hugged me. When I said that was unnatural, he called me slut.

The Baron paused and told me to get up.

I found I was quivering.

Hearing him unzip, I looked down to see his cock pale and hard in his hand—it was longer and sleeker than any I'd seen: a beautiful sex, a perfect sex, and oh, how firm. Longing to lick and pleasure him, I began to sink to my knees, but he grabbed me by the hair. "No, Anita." Raising me by the curls, he stretched me back. I had to relent. He glanced down at my corset, streaked with the remnants of another's pleasure, and with his lips curling back against his teeth and a wildness in the blacks of his eyes, he cupped my slippery breast.

"You need this," I said to him.

His smile curled up at one corner, and I caught a drift of the scent on his neck. Suddenly, he thrust me back so I pressed against the dresser, my pot of cold cream crashing to the floor, and he was on me in a second, pushing me back against the mirror, which thumped, collapsing, so my back stuck to the glass. He thrust his hands deep between my thighs, and at my ear, hissed, "I want you, Anita." I cried out. His sex ground mine, and he tore through the lace. He filled me from shaft to tip. I jolted on the dresser so the mirror thudded behind me and a bottle crashed and broke, sending out a rosy scent. I was so wet that his thrusts were smooth as oil, and my sex, unused to the shape of a man, tingled and stretched. Through his teeth, he said my slit was tight as a virgin's.

I'd never heard it called that—a *slit*.

He said to call him Papa, but instead I cried, "Oh, Uncle..." and thought I could cry it forever.

There, plowing his sex into mine, with the dressing table shunting at the wall, I glanced into the angled mirror that stood in the corner. And with my stockinged thighs wrapped around the thrusting Baron, my heeled sandals glinting and my red lips stretched apart, I, Anita, exotic dancer, released an ecstatic yell and finally learned to give way.

For seven weeks, the Baron watched my act and came to me afterward to force my compliance. As I pleasured the men onstage, I felt I could sense his stare, and I knew, unlike the others who cried out and groaned, the Baron would be sitting still, patiently blazing. I'd always find him in my dressing room, where he'd sometimes bind my wrists and fuck me from behind or make me suck him while calling him "Uncle," or come across my bosom so my cleavage dripped not only with his fluid but that of a stranger. But though it was savage, it was also kind. I'd walk from the theater with a lightness of step I'd never experienced before. I ate keenly; food had new flavor. Champagne bubbles now danced on my tongue. I'd grow drunk more quickly than before. When new shoes pinched me, I reveled in the pain.

Then, one evening, he didn't turn up.

I'd always known he'd leave.

I mourned on the stool by my dressing table, dabbing my streaked mascara with a cotton ball, staring emptily into the mirror that had cracked from tumbling so often. Even then, I guessed, he was forcing a different woman to relent; one who, like me, had been cut off from the world. But something about that knowledge made me reach for my clit and touch myself afresh.

"Uncle, Uncle!" I began to cry.

I never really stopped.

CHLORINE

Amelia Thornton

I can feel you watching me, devouring me with your eyes. My body is stretched across a raft, floating lazily in the middle of the pool in our suite. My fingertips are trailing in the water, leaving little ripples as I drift past, and every so often I will dip my foot in and push myself off in a different direction. I seem oblivious to your gaze, wrapped up in my own little world, but I know you are looking at me. We have been here several days already, but my skin is still as white as always, sharply contrasting with the cherry red I have painted my toenails and the black of my hair, damp with chlorine. My swimsuit, red with tiny white polka dots, barely hides the deep, crisscrossing lines from where you caned me last night; my eyes are hidden behind red heart-shaped sunglasses. Nobody here knows you or me or what we are. Do they think I'm your daughter? Your son's girlfriend? Your niece? Or do they know I'm your lover, just not in what way you love me?

I appear to be bored now, bored with just lying here, sun

scorching my soft skin, so I plunge myself into the cool water and swim to the side. I can feel you watching me climb out, my wet hair sticking to my skin, rivulets of water running down my back, droplets clinging to the curve in the small of my back, trailing across the swell of my breasts. Languidly, I walk to my lounger, so casual, almost as if I've not even noticed you sitting there. But I have. The terra-cotta tiles are hot from being under the sun all day, and my steps leave little wet footprints on them, the soles of my feet burning, the heat of the air filling my lungs in the way that only ever seems to happen in exotic, far-off places. I like that feeling.

You're pretending to read now, or maybe you really are reading. But I know you will keep stealing glances at me, as I twist my wet hair on top of my head, stretch myself backward, take a sip of my drink. You will look like you're not looking, like your book really is that engrossing, but I know you better than that. I have ordered a milkshake from room service, a really good milkshake, with bright paper cocktail umbrellas and a twisty straw and three glacé cherries on top. Each long, slow suck of the straw between my lips, painted the same red as my nails; each time I drag the straw out, covered in whipped cream, and lick the length of it; each time, I'm thinking of you watching me, thinking of what I want you to do to me. I pick out a cherry with my fingers and tilt my head back, gripping the fruit between my teeth as I pull the stalk off, twist my tongue around it, feel the chill of frothy milk and sickly sweet syrup slipping down my throat. Every taste bud seems amplified, each sensation unbearably sensual, performing for you yet lost in myself.

I'm so engrossed in my little flirtation show, I almost don't notice as you slam your book shut, put it down and firmly, decisively, begin to walk toward me. Suddenly I'm a little scared, my heart beating that little bit quicker, wondering what it is you're going to do to me, wondering if I've gone too far again. You stop, standing above me so powerful, so authoritative, your shadow falling across me, making me look up from my milk-shake to meet your gaze.

"Kirsten?"

"Y-yes, ma'am?"

"Are you not forgetting something?"

My mind is racing, mentally cycling through every possible thing you could have asked me to do this afternoon. It couldn't have been to make your coffee, just the way you like it, seeing as we have room service. It couldn't have been to polish your shoes, or iron your best silk blouse, or ensure your favorite lavender scent was spritzed on every last item of your undergar-ments, as I did all of that last night. Surely I could not have been so foolish as to neglect my duties, while lucky enough to be here in this paradise with you? So I just stay silent, hoping you will enlighten me. You don't.

"Well, since you clearly have not paid any attention to a word I've been saying the whole time we've been here, perhaps you need a little reminder. What do you think?"

Your voice is so calm, the way it always is when you are about to punish me, the way that always sends shivers down my spine, even when I know it means you are going to hurt me. I cannot possibly imagine what it is I've forgotten, but that seems irrelevant now, as you wait for me to move into position, wait for me to give myself to you to discipline. Awkwardly, I get to my feet, allow you to sit yourself more comfortably on the lounger, squirm with discomfort as you gently pat your lap to motion me across it. There is something about over-the-knee spankings that simultaneously horrifies and excites me—the childish humiliation, the ungainly positioning, the exposure of my bottom making it so easy for you to smack. No matter how naughty I have been or how cross you are with me, it always manages to make me wet.

I reluctantly bend myself across your knee, wriggling just slightly in the way I know looks enticing, a tiny spark of excitement coursing through me as I think of how much enjoyment you gain from humiliating me. Even when you're disciplining me for bad behavior, it always turns me on to think of you gaining pleasure from punishing me—and I know, no matter what you say, or how angry you look, you're always just as wet as me.

The first smack still makes me jump, even though I'm expecting it. The moment your hand meets my waiting flesh, the sound as surfaces collide, is always the best part for me, the promise of what is to come contained in that one strike. Slowly you continue, sharp swats of your hand meticulously applied across my cheerful polka dots, not even hurting yet but hard enough to let me know it will. You pause, your hand resting softly on the damp fabric, as if thinking.

"Take them off."

"Are you kidding me? Oh, please don't! We're outside! Somebody might see!" I whine, the thought of my bare bottom exposed to any pool boy that happens to come strolling by just too unbearable to even think of.

"Do you not think it will be embarrassing enough for them to see you bent over my knee like a naughty girl?" you respond dryly, clearly not caring a jot whether anyone sees me exposed or not. "I doubt they'll be noticing whether you have your swimsuit on or not! Now don't make me tell you again, otherwise a spanking will be the least of your worries."

Resentfully, I get to my feet and clumsily push the bikini bottom to my midthigh before positioning myself back across your lap, my skin prickling as it is exposed to the warm afternoon air. You're right, I suppose, that just being caught being spanked would be embarrassing enough, never mind it being on my bare bottom. You're always right, much to my misfortune at times. Satisfied with my reluctantly presented backside, you continue with an air of determination, each strike becoming decidedly more ferocious until I find myself gasping, just a little, at the strength of it, my toes twisting together as I try to distract myself, my eyes squeezed tight shut until—

"Please!"

You pause, your hand midair, poised to launch.

"Excuse me?"

"Please, ma'am, you're hurting me!"

You laugh, that laugh of utter ridicule I have come to expect when I say something as ludicrously obvious as that. I still always find myself saying it though, like a ritual, a well-played game, where we know our lines and our cues but still are surprised when the plot twists come in.

"I know," you sigh, and I know you will be smiling. "I know I'm hurting you, Kirsten, but sometimes I just need to do what's necessary to remind you. You don't want to be a bad girl for me, do you?"

"No, ma'am, not at all!"

"So perhaps you should quiet down and stop making such a fuss; otherwise I may have to go indoors and fetch that nice wooden paddle you like so much, and you don't want that, I'm sure."

"No, ma'am, no, I don't! I'll try harder, I promise."

"Good."

I bite my lip to crush my squeals as you smack me harder, your girl who tries to be good but still needs taking in hand sometimes, who needs a sound spanking to set her back on the right path once more. But I know I could never live without it, without this, without you. That feeling of complete calm that comes over me when I surrender to you, when you take from me what is yours, is incomparable to anything I've felt in any other relationship, to anything I've felt in life, I guess. It just makes everything seem so simple; all of the worries of mundane, everyday existence fading away to be replaced with such clear, definable goals of completing the tasks you set me and submitting to your wishes with complete devotion. You are the yin to my yang, the other half of all the sides of me. How I love you, my wicked queen.

But before I even know it, you have stopped and are quietly ordering me to my feet. Awkwardly, I stand before you, feeling your gaze upon me, my face flushed with embarrassment, my eyes unsure where to look. Do you even know what it is you do to me? Do you even know that every time you look at me, I still get that feeling in my head like I've just reached the top of the roller coaster, and I know the drop is right there waiting? I think you do know. I think that's why you choose to push me off, every time.

You take my hand and bring me to kneel before you, my skin hot against burnt terra-cotta, my face almost next to yours now, taking in the scent of coconut shampoo and sticky sunblock, chlorine and wet hair. The sun has brought out the freckles on the bridge of my nose, making the seductive red lipstick look somehow ridiculous in comparison, but you cannot seem to stop looking at me, your eyes drinking in every feature of my face, as if preserving this one little moment in time forever, this one little mental image. My heart is pounding, feeling your closeness, your intensity. I want to kiss you right now more than I have ever wanted anything in my life.

So I do. I lean in, my mouth so close to yours I can inhale your breath, my fingertips against your cheekbone, my lips brushing yours almost shyly as I wait for you to respond. No matter how many times I kiss you, it always makes my stomach drop when you abandon your cool restraint and just pull me into you, when your tongue pushes between my teeth, your fingers twisting in my hair, for once losing a fraction of your control. The intimacy suffocates me as you drown me in your kisses, hungry for me, as if tearing me apart with your lips and tongue and teeth, flooding me with all the desire you keep trapped inside you in your everyday life, your life so hardened by so many years of self-composure.

"Get inside."

Wordlessly I scurry after you, following your purposeful steps through the wide French doors to our suite, admiring the way your hair falls over your shoulders, the lines of your body beneath your thin cotton sundress. I could spend all day just running my hands across your skin, feeling the softness of your hair between my fingers, kissing your earlobes and eyelids and every single part of you.... The crisp white sheets of our bed are still tangled from this morning's tryst, pillows haphazardly tossed to the floor in the heat of lust, somehow making your regal beauty stand out even more as you lay yourself back amongst piles of immaculate white cotton. Like a cat I crawl up next to you, pressing my lips against your hot skin, my hands tugging at the fabric of your dress, pulling it away from your body, smiling as you childishly wriggle out of it. My mouth is on yours again instantly, my tongue running along the inside of your teeth, almost wanting to climb inside your mouth and completely lose myself in there. I trail tiny kisses across your cheek, feeling your breathing grow heavy and needy as my lips close around the soft lobe of your ear, sucking it gently, my fingers twisting in your hair, until at last you hoarsely whisper the words you know I love to hear.

"Fuck me."

I smile at your need, your desire for me, for my hands, for

my mouth. The thought of that tiny glimmer of control over you makes my head spin, you who control me so absolutely with just a single word. At times like this, I want to make you wait, like you make me, but I never can. My fingers are inside you before I can even consider anything else, your wetness sucking me in and surrounding me with heat, a low moan escaping your lips as I fill you with feeling. Your eyes close as I rhythmically curl my fingers deeper into you, your hands gripping tightly to the bedsheets as you push yourself up farther and allow me to enter you harder and faster, pounding almost, the way I know you need but you never know how to ask for. I gaze at your delicate features, the sheen of sweat glistening on the stretched tendons of your neck, wishing I could touch you everywhere at once but knowing I can't. Instinctively my mouth draws toward your clit, enveloping it in my lips, sucking it and kissing it and tracing my tongue in tiny circles around it, feeling your thighs tighten around my upper body, pinning me inescapably into you. But I would never want to escape.

I can feel your body growing rigid and tense, building toward your release, and I cannot help but inwardly smile to myself at how beautiful you are when you surrender like this. With renewed passion I push deeper into you, my tongue dancing on your clit, almost physically experiencing the intensity inside you as you climb higher and higher. Like an animal, you tear my hair with your hands as you fall off the edge, a strangled cry escaping your throat, just for those few, brief seconds completely outside yourself yet completely within yourself at the same time. Tenderly I disentangle my limbs from yours, delicately kissing your agonizingly sensitive clit as I crawl up to lie in your arms, your breathing still pounding in your chest as I lay my head upon you. We stay like that for what seems like forever, word-lessly close, until finally I speak.

"Please, ma'am...what was it I forgot to do for you? I tried so hard to remember everything...."

You laugh softly, almost as if you'd forgotten the entire episode yourself.

"Oh, you didn't forget anything. I just wanted to see you in trouble, that's all. You're always so adorable when you think you've been naughty."

Gently, you kiss the top of my head and squeeze your arms tighter around me. I want to be your captive forever.

RAINBOW NIGHT

Giselle Renarde

Adele spun her ring around her finger until the heavy princess-cut diamond faced the room. It was so new she hadn't taken it to be resized yet. How predictable of Elliot not to know her ring size, even after so many years and so much jewelry. But how could she complain? At least he had the foresight to have his assistant remind him when their anniversary rolled around and in time to have their jeweler set aside something rare and exclusive. No, her sole complaint this evening was that neither Sissy nor Hue had taken notice of her new treasure.

Ahem. Adele cleared her throat just loudly enough to draw Sissy's attention from the male-dominated conversation. Hue, with her MBA and her crossbred Vietnamese-Manhattan accent, glanced briefly in Adele's direction before rejoining the market talk.

She tried again. "Did nobody notice the ring Elliot bought me?"

Even the husbands ceased their self-important ramblings to

turn their attention to Adele's diamond. Hue's expression turned lovey-dovey as she nursed her lemon fizz. The woman was tough as nails in business but always a sucker for romance. "Was that for your anniversary?" she cooed. "How nice." Poking her husband in the ribs, she chuckled, "This one's always buying me cars."

"Impressive," Sissy agreed, with a deliberate glance in Adele's direction. "A ring that big would look terribly gaudy on me, but I've always said the look suits older women rather well." And with a saccharine smile, she set her third cosmopolitan down and folded her hands in her Chanel-clad lap.

Normally, Adele might have been peeved, but the new gift put her in a refreshingly giving mood. *Just look at the poor girl's bare fingers!* she thought. Sissy claimed to prefer the cleaner look of her shard-studded engagement ring and plain-Jane wedding band, but even those outside their circle knew Roger's capital was dwindling. Rumor had it Sissy'd even been spotted shopping in a discount supermarket. And Adele had a sneaking suspicion the bottle of Domaine Bouchard Père & Fils she'd brought to dinner last week was in fact a Cuvée Saint-Pierre with a false label pasted on.

How the mighty had fallen.

It was Sissy's Roger who broke the silence. "Well, I think your ring is as lovely as you are, Adele." Coming from anyone else, that might have been a shot, but Roger was rather too stupid to come up with clever quips. Pretty, though. One of those Harvard boys who never aged a day over twenty-one.

"Yes," Pat chimed in. Hue's husband was eerily intelligent, but he never said much. "Congratulations to you both."

And then the conversation drifted back to the stock market and everything that was boring in the world of the elite. How tiresome her friends had grown—her husband along with them, if she was being honest. Had they always been so dull, or had her perspective simply evolved over time? She was hostess. It was her duty to save the evening from the depths of dreariness. "Let's play a game!" she called out, raising her brandy in the air as she rose from her Art Shoppe chair.

Again, she caught nobody's attention but Sissy's. "What sort of game?"

Adele hadn't thought that far ahead. "I don't know, really. Backgammon?"

Sissy didn't even reply before turning her gaze in Elliot's direction as he went on and on about Dubai. If only she read newspapers or had something insightful to contribute. It didn't even have to be news, just some piece of information that would capture everybody's imagination.

"You know what I heard?" Adele cut in. She asked the question loudly enough to draw everybody's eyes. "I saw a report on television...it's really quite shameful, you know...it was about these parties children are having...rainbow parties, I think they were called."

Hue let out a cackle before covering her mouth with her hand. "That wasn't a news report, that was on one of those trashy daytime talk shows."

"Oh...was it?"

"Where do you find time to watch trashy daytime talk shows?" Pat asked his wife.

"I don't," Hue said. "I just happened to see a commercial for the program when I was watching *Law & Order*."

Pat raised his eyebrows, but said nothing.

"At any rate," Adele went on, sensing a conversational shift away from her topic of interest. "Apparently these teenaged kids get together for what amount to blow job parties. The girls all wear different lipsticks, and the boys aim to get their penises painted in every shade."

"There's a thing or two we can learn from kids today," Elliot said with a smirk. Adele smiled back at him. He had a very kind air about him when he thought about sex.

"Not that kids should be doing it…" Hue said, at first seeming like she might write off the whole conversation as perverse. After a sip of her lemon fizz, she changed gears. "But the idea…the idea is…intriguing…"

Roger chuckled, setting a firm hand on Sissy's knee. "And I thought we were inventive in our day!"

"I don't think that's very funny," Sissy said, smacking his hand away. "Those poor girls! Subjected to such humiliations!"

Elliot tapped Adele lightly on her finger, and then gave her a look that seemed to say, *Poor Roger!*

"What do you have against cocksucking?" Hue asked the willowy blonde on the couch. "Don't tell me you refuse to give head."

Sissy crossed and uncrossed her ankles. Roger answered for her. "She gives it," he said. His voice wavered. "Under duress…"

Hue, Adele and Elliot chuckled while Pat took a sip of scotch. Lowering her gaze, Sissy reached for the cosmopolitan she'd placed on the table. She mimed drinking even though it was very apparent there was nothing left in her glass. "Can I get you another?" Adele asked. She liked Sissy better drunk, but for such a slight girl it took a considerable amount of alcohol to get her there.

"Oh…" Sissy said. Her voice was high and strained, like she was going to cry. "Okay…"

"Why don't you like sucking cock?" Hue prodded. She didn't appear to be teasing Sissy, only curious about the younger woman's hang-ups. "Men love it, you know. Ask your husband. Roger, you love a good blow job, don't you?"

Roger glanced with shifty eyes at his wife before agreeing. "More than anything."

"Really?" Sissy asked, looking at Roger and then quickly looking away. "It's only that his thing is so big. It makes me gag," she explained to Hue as Adele handed her another drink. "Thank you."

Leaning back in the sofa with a self-satisfied grin, Roger placed an arm around Sissy and pulled her in close. He opened his mouth as though he were about to say something but then seemed lost for words.

"How big is big?" Hue asked. Her voice sounded strange and deep. With slow and deliberate motions, she zipped open her purse and pulled out a tube of lipstick and a mirror. "Hold this," she instructed her husband, placing the lid in his hand before pressing deep burgundy gloss against her lips. Her eyes didn't waver from the mirror. Everybody else's eyes were on her, too. When she'd coated her full lips with a surge of color, she smacked them together and smiled at Pat. From the chair beside the sofa, he gave her the lid. Before taking it, she asked, "What do you think?"

"Looks very nice," Pat replied. "Dark."

Hue turned to the man sitting beside her on the couch. She smiled, looking past him to Sissy at the other end of the sofa. "Maybe a smaller cock would suit you better. Maybe you'd enjoy giving head if you could simply savor the texture without getting your throat torn open."

Adele stared across the room with a combination of apprehension, disbelief and exhilaration. "Would anybody like another drink?" she asked before Sissy could respond.

Nobody but Sissy could be distracted from the tension building on the couch, and she simply shook her head. And then, as Elliot squirmed in his chair, Sissy reached for her bag and brought out a tube of cotton candy–pink lipstick. Her first coat had been all but lost to her cosmopolitan glass. She embellished her soft pink lips with a generous coat of light, waxy lipstick and then smacked them together.

The whole room seemed to be smiling with unspoken knowledge. "My lipstick," Adele said. "It's in my bedroom." Without another word, she bolted up the stairs and grasped a tube of bright red lipstick. She watched herself in the mirror as she put it on. Why had she taken it to heart when Sissy called her old? She wasn't that at all. Adele looked as vibrant as she had in college. Though she'd never been what one might call "pretty," she was certainly a striking woman. And Elliot still found her attractive, if his anniversary gift was any indication.

By the time Adele returned to the parlor, the husbands had moved to the sofa. All three sat side by side—there were Roger's blond curls, Pat's chestnut brown hair and Elliot's salt and pepper on the end. She stared at the backs of their heads before gazing up at Sissy sitting in the chair Adele had abandoned, and Hue perched on its arm. They looked at Adele as if to ask permission. That was her impression, at least until she circled the sofa to find her husband's belt unbuckled and fly unzipped. His familiar cock sat limp outside the pin-striped gabardine slacks she'd picked out for him. Adele bought all her husband's clothes. Had Sissy selected Roger's deep blue dress pants? And had Hue purchased Pat's impeccably creased black trousers? They were all so well dressed and all owing to the women behind the men. Without their wives, the boys would flounder in all things. The women held the power.

Try as she might, Adele couldn't keep herself from peeking at the half-hard cock poking out of Roger's fly. Sissy was right—it was big. Not frighteningly huge, but certainly a good size. On the slim side, in fact, but long and curving to the right as though it were reaching for his hand. It leapt like an excited dog's tail as it waited for action.

Pat's dick rested still against his thigh, quietly drooling precome onto the black fabric of his trousers. Pat had a fat cock. It was hard to tell just by looking, but his girth seemed to surpass Roger's or even Elliot's, for that matter. Elliot had a very middle-of-the-road cock. Adele had always thought so. It wasn't big, but it wasn't small. It was neither fat nor thin. She knew what to expect of it, and it delivered each time. To see it set like the third place recipient against their friends' winning cocks, she almost felt sorry for her husband, though she didn't know why. It really was a very pleasant dick.

"Well?" Hue said. "Are we going to sit here staring at our husbands' pricks all night, or are we going to get down and dirty?"

The business world had rendered Hue shameless, but Adele felt a blush coming on. Sissy simply sat staring. At what? Her eyes were glazed over, likely in delayed response to the evening's many cosmopolitans. "How do we decide," Sissy said in a small voice, "who starts where?"

"We should all start with our own husbands, shouldn't we?" Adele said, not knowing where to look. She tried to stare at her manicure, but her eyes kept wandering back to the line of growing penises on the couch.

The husbands sat still as strip club patrons—not that Adele had ever set foot inside a strip club...but she'd heard things. They seemed to avoid looking at each other's laps, or accidentally touching thighs. A childhood memory flashed before Adele's eyes, of waiting in line for vaccines at school. The whole class had fallen silent in wait. Even the class clown was too nervous to rouse their spirits.

Rising from the chair where Sissy sat like a lobotomy victim,

Hue approached the couch like a jaguar. "I say we finish off with our husbands rather than start with them."

"Oh. Really?" Adele disagreed, but she didn't want to admit the reason why. Different men's come tasted different, she'd heard. Elliot's wasn't awful, but it wasn't the most appetizing substance on Earth. She wouldn't mind tasting somebody else's, for comparison.

Pat began to fidget, until his leg brushed Elliot's and then Roger's. The boys on the ends tried to squirm closer to the sofa's arms, but they were already as close as they were going to get. All three laughed with nerves. Now they obviously didn't know what to do with their hands. Set them on their thighs? Cross their arms? Fold them behind their heads?

Sissy emerged from her alcohol-induced stupor to toss her hair back with a critical cackle. "Oh, give it a rest, boys." Crawling over the coffee table, she tumbled to the floor at Pat's feet. "Touching thighs won't make you gay."

Without another word, spoken or implied, Sissy held her blonde curls back with her fingertips and leaned toward Hue's husband's fat cock. For a moment, she hovered above it, seeming not to know what to do. Her breath on Pat's exposed skin obviously excited the man, because he tossed his head back and let out a deep groan. His untouched dick surged forward to whack Sissy's lips, and she burbled with amusement.

"Pat's prick is after you, Sissy," Hue chuckled. "Better open wide and say 'ah!'"

The whole room watched as the pretty blonde sucked Pat's cockhead between her lips. He groaned, placing his hands on the back of her head and pulling her forward until his entire cock was lodged in her mouth. Sissy didn't even sputter. She sucked in until her cheeks went gaunt and then pulled away to see if she'd left pink lipstick along the top of his shaft. She had.

Adele was too mesmerized to note the others' reactions.

Desire overwhelmed her senses, and before she could stop herself, she'd knelt down in front of Roger. His cock grew like a spring shoot when she took it in hand. Adele loved the feel of a hard cock in her grasp, like silk over steel. Roger's cock. Sissy's Roger. However cute he was, she didn't want to look up at him. She didn't want to know whether he was looking down on her with tenderness, or curiosity, or lust or disgust. Instead, she stared at his tip as it eased out liquid.

Tugging slowly on Roger's shaft, Adele licked the nectar of the gods. It tasted salty; like Elliot's, but different. Wrapping her fist around the base of his dick, she lunged at him. Surprise attack! She sucked him in corkscrew motion, twisting her head as she ate his long cock. His skin felt warm and grateful against her tongue. She went wild on him. She held tight to his shaft as she plunged again and again. Holding him with both hands, she set her red lips around his cockhead and sucked the precome from the tip like water through a straw.

And then she heard a moan: Elliot.

Still gripping Roger's dick, Adele looked up and over the blonde head buried in Pat's lap. Apparently Sissy did like sucking cock if the size was right, but the pretty young thing was not her primary concern. Hue had her hands inside Elliot's shirt, grasping at his slight paunch as she held his cock between dark lips. A surge of possessiveness shot through Adele as she watched. Hue was a demon of the boardroom, a vixen of the bedroom and superior to Adele in every way conceivable. But not in this. Adele would prove her abilities.

Releasing Roger's reddened dick, Adele crawled over Sissy's bent form and urged Hue away from her husband. "My turn," Adele said, reapplying her lipstick to coat her husband's purple cock red. "You try Roger. Leave Sissy with Pat. She seems to have found a penis she likes."

Hue glared down at the girl hunched over her husband's crotch, feeding like a calf at its mother's teat. Her expression softened as she watched. She nodded and said, "Perfect," as she raced around the coffee table to fall at Roger's feet.

"We meet again," Elliot said with a silly smirk.

Leaning down, Adele kissed his lips, leaving red marks in her wake. "Isn't this just nutty?"

He took her wrists and folded Adele's hands around his hard cock smeared with burgundy lipstick. His eager smile took her back to college days. "Do you want to go down on me?"

Adele giggled like a schoolgirl. "I don't know," she teased. "I guess. I mean, if that's what you want...."

With a grin, she licked his shaft from root to tip. It tasted fruity—Hue's lipstick. Adele hesitated for a moment. Hue's lips had encircled her husband's cock. When Adele enclosed his hard shaft in her mouth, she'd be sucking Hue's saliva along with Elliot's gleaming precome.

"What's the holdup?" he asked over Roger's and Pat's sighs and Hue's deep moans as she devoured another husband's dick. Elliot fluffed Adele's hair with his fingers as she looked up into his eyes. He was hers, now and forever. Who cared about Hue? It was just a blow job.

Without another word, she lunged on Elliot's erection. Digging his balls from his jockeys, she gripped them the way he liked it. He tossed his head back and sighed with the other men. Adele took his shaft between her lips and ate it until she gagged. She couldn't manage the whole thing. She never could. But that didn't stop her trying. Her fingers formed a cock ring as she teased him with her tongue. The size of his erection told her how much he loved what she was doing.

"Oh, lord, I'm going to come!"

Adele looked up to see Roger shaking his head left to right as

Hue lunged at his cock. She sucked him off at the speed of light. That boy didn't stand a chance! He bucked up into her throat and she took it with pleasured moans. Though her eyes ran wet with tears, she threw her head into his thrusting lap until he gripped her long black hair and held her perfectly still. Neither moved. Still, Adele could hear Hue's wet sucking noises as she finished him off.

Now Sissy wouldn't get a chance to paint her husband pink. Maybe she didn't want to. She had her arms wrapped around Pat's middle like a child with a security blanket. His cock was her baby bottle. "Do you want to trade?" Adele asked her. "You can have Elliot, if you'd like to try him."

Elliot laughed. "Pass me around the room, why don't you!"

Sissy turned her head to look at Elliot's dick while Adele fondled his balls. "He's got red and purple already," Adele said. "He just needs pink to complete the rainbow."

With a subdued giggle, Sissy planted a sweet pink kiss against Pat's plump cock before agreeing. Hue had settled into Adele's chair like the Queen of the Nile by the time Adele and Sissy reapplied their lipstick and traded places. In truth, Adele was looking forward to playing with Pat's cock. She liked that it was shorter than the rest. Maybe she could fit the whole thing in her mouth. There was an element of satisfaction in the idea.

She tried to think of something amusing to say to Hue's shy husband, but her brain was fried on cocksucking. A meek, "Hi," was all she could manage, and then she felt silly for saying something so inane. "I'll just...do this..."

Pat said, "Okay," and then followed that up with, "Thanks."

Shaking her head, Adele advised herself to say nothing further.

The base of Pat's cock was veritably slathered in pink lipstick.

When she wrapped her mouth around his fat cock, she could have sworn she tasted cosmopolitans. She was right—the whole thing fit. It came close to gagging her, but not close enough. Letting Pat's erection slide almost all the way out of her mouth, she trapped his wide cockhead between her red lips. She let her tongue dance along his satin-smooth tip as it pumped salty precome inside her mouth. He nearly jumped onto Roger's sleeping lap when she tickled the slit. She never truly understood how sensitive men's cockheads were. Was any part of her body so sensitive? How could she ever compare? It was impossible to know.

Pat's cock didn't have the length for her usual trick of wrapping her fist around the shaft as she sucked the tip. Anyway, it felt good to swallow a cock whole. So, she did what Sissy had done before her and wrapped her arms around his middle. When her clothed tits touched his thighs, she pressed her body hard against his. Pat didn't move. As in conversation, he didn't say much. He simply sat there and took it all in. That's the one thing Adele didn't care for—his lack of enthusiasm. Now he was a challenge. She had to make him come.

When Elliot's familiar pre-ejaculatory noises met Adele's ears, she wanted to look up at him. She wanted to see what little Sissy was doing to her husband that made him moan and squeal. Even his hips writhed beneath the girl—Adele could feel him moving beside her. But she didn't look up. Her husband's joy only urged her to bring Pat to orgasm as quickly as she could.

Holding Pat's cockhead between her lips, Adele snuck her index and middle fingers on either side of his shaft. She held that fat dick between her fingers like a firm, fleshy cigarette. Keeping tight suction on his tip, she ran her fingers up and down the saliva and lipstick path from the root of his cock up to her lips and back down again. She stroked him fast. It was all she could think to do, and it worked. Pat sighed. His hips urged his fat cock farther into her mouth, and she took it. She took it all in again, and this time he seemed to appreciate it all the more. He thrust his hips. She sucked his cock. She sucked the whole damn thing. She sucked it until Pat shrieked and hissed and thrust his hips beneath her.

He came in her mouth, and she swallowed his hot cream as fast as she could. It tasted salty and almost tangy. Even with all of her culinary expertise, it was hard to describe the taste of come.

When she rose from the floor, she didn't look Pat in the eye. Nerves made her chuckle, but her chest felt tight until Elliot grabbed her by the wrist. He'd already folded his cock neatly into his pants and zipped up his fly. Sissy had taken a seat on the arm of Hue's chair. In that moment, despite the two other cocksuckers in the room, despite the two other men with lipsticks on their dipsticks, Adele felt perfectly alone with her husband.

Elliot pulled Adele into his lap and kissed her lips. With a laugh, he said, "You taste like come." As the others chuckled along, Elliot whispered, "Some way to spend a wedding anniversary."

Adele nestled her head against his shoulder and smiled.

FRESH CANVAS

Donna George Storey

Miranda reached toward the buzzer on the imposing oak door, imagining for a moment that her hand belonged to a stranger. The flesh looked so pale and clean, the nails impeccably manicured. Such a dainty hand should never be defiled by the unspeakable things she was about to do.

She paused, her arm poised in midair like a dancing nymph in a Renaissance painting. Suddenly her fingers seemed to swell and blush, glistening with a dewy sheen.

Greedy slut!

Miranda inhaled and stabbed the doorbell with her index finger.

Sam opened the door with a smile. He always seemed to dress so nicely for these occasions—pressed khakis and a forest green shirt that looked expensive, touchable.

"Good evening, Miranda. May I take your wrap?"

She nodded and eased her coat into his waiting arms.

His old-fashioned courtesy made her want to laugh. Then

again he'd always been the perfect gentleman-pervert. Back in college, he'd squired her to the town's best restaurants for weeks, apparently desiring nothing more than a good night kiss. When he finally invited her back to his dorm room, the first thing he did was tie her hands to his bunk bed with her own panty hose. Then he fucked her with the lights on and made her gaze into his eyes when she came.

For the six months they were together, he could get her sopping wet just by giving her that same penetrating stare.

Tonight Sam's expression was impassive as he took in her tailored gray business suit and crisp white blouse. When his eyes settled on the large bag she carried, he smiled again.

"We have eight tonight," he said. "You're getting quite the reputation, Miranda."

"Thanks to you."

"On the contrary. I'm merely the discreet host."

"You have the paperwork for the new ones?"

"You can always trust me to have everything in proper order."

Miranda pursed her lips. The words *men* and *trust* weren't exactly a happy couple in her mind these days. She had to admit, however, that Sam had managed everything flawlessly from the very beginning. She inclined her head, ever so slightly, and said, "I'll go get ready now."

"Do you need any help?" His eyes glittered.

"I'll call you when it's time to put on the blindfold," she said over her shoulder.

The guest room was much the same as she'd left it the week before. A single bed occupied the center of the room like a raft floating on a lake. Today it was fitted out in deep red satin. The sheet was clean but the glossy shine was already fading. She wondered, with a flicker of a smile, how many times it had been washed in the last month.

Miranda undressed, hanging her suit carefully in the closet and arranging her underwear over hangers as well. Next she emptied the bag on the bed: a peach satin Christian Dior negligee, a box of dental dams, a pearl necklace, the scarf she'd use as her blindfold.

She could feel her breath coming faster.

Trying her best to keep her hands steady, she draped the pearls around her neck and fastened the clasp. They were a wedding gift from Tom's mother. As she shimmied into the floor-length negligee, slit to the thighs on each side, she remembered the leer on Tom's face when he gave it to her. She forgot exactly when, probably some Valentine's Day back when he made more money than she did. Both items were expensive. At one time she'd even treasured them.

They'd be all too easy to let go of now.

Miranda glanced at herself in the full-length mirror. Again she felt as if she were observing a stranger's body. The woman standing before her was thin, a melancholy Modigliani rather than a winsome Botticelli. Yet her breasts were still perky and her skin had a rosy glow in the golden lamplight. All in all, she wasn't too bad for thirty-eight. It helped, no doubt, that she worked out regularly and had never had kids.

Sometimes disappointments work out for the best in the end.

Miranda pushed open the guest room door. "Sam?"

"Be right there," he called from the kitchen. She thought she caught the clink of ice in a tumbler. She suspected they all enjoyed a cocktail or two to loosen up beforehand. She, on the other hand, liked to stay sharp so she could drink in every last sensation.

She sat on the bed, the scarf in her lap. Sam walked in

purposefully and sat down next to her. Sliding the silk from her hands, he tied it around her eyes with expert skill.

Everything was blank now. The way she liked it.

Sam lingered at her side. She could smell the whisky on his breath.

"Any special requests tonight?" he asked.

"I'm quite satisfied with the usual."

"I noticed." He leaned in closer. "You know, Miranda, you've always been lovely, but since you started coming here for your...treatments...you've positively blossomed."

Miranda stiffened. It wasn't that she didn't love hearing men's compliments, their intimate confessions of desire. It was one of the reasons she was here tonight. But this was too early, too sweet.

"I've learned a few things since college," he continued, resting a warm hand on her shoulder. "Can you stay tonight?"

She swallowed, fighting the urge to shrug him away. Yet deep in her belly, her secret muscles contracted almost painfully, hungry for a taste of him and his new tricks.

She hadn't expected the evening to get so sticky this soon.

At that moment the doorbell rang. They both jumped guiltily, which amused Miranda, because Sam's proposition was doubtless the most respectable interaction she'd have with a man tonight.

"I guess they couldn't wait to see you." Sam pulled his hand away. But he seemed to be waiting for her reply.

"Don't be rude to our guests," she murmured.

The bed creaked in disappointment as he rose. "It's a standing offer," he added and pulled the door closed behind him.

She was alone again, relieved but oddly restless. Yet before long she'd have plenty of company.

Miranda stretched out on the bed, wriggling to get in a

comfortable position. The scritch-scratch of the plastic sheet beneath the satin made her own skin prickle.

Already the room was palpably warmer.

Blindness sharpened her other senses, too. She heard Sam greet the new visitors. One voice was familiar, a cheery, joking baritone. The other offered a rumbling introduction and his name, a fake one perhaps? Miranda herself had no name now. In this room, she was only "she" or "her." She had no idea what they called her out there, to each other, or in their minds as they blocked out a few hours on Thursday evening for a happy hour "client meeting."

There'd be five more, if they all came.

They always did.

Miranda had Facebook to thank for her new secret life. Searching for the names of old friends and lovers was the perfect way to spend a sleepless night. Eventually she worked back through the years to Sam, who wore his age well in his profile picture, his "single" status as alluring as the fact he lived in the same city. Miranda sent off a mildly provocative message. He responded. Two weeks later—and eighteen years after the last time he trussed her up to his bunk bed—they were chatting over cock-tails at the Bourbon & Branch.

Coincidentally, Sam was going through a divorce, too. They'd both suffered the same indignity: spouses running off with colleagues at the office. But Sam at least had the comfort of a cliché, Miranda had complained to him as the second brandied apple took effect. His wife had gone off with her rich boss. Her rival was older and positively dowdy. Tom said she had a "warm heart," but that was clearly code for big tits that had lost the battle with gravity. And he was taking on two young stepkids in the bargain, which was no kind of trade-up at all.

"He doesn't deserve you," Sam declared, a twinkle in his eye.

"Obviously not. But I'm the one left alone in that cold, empty house. I don't want love now. Maybe never again. But I want—I crave—warmth."

She felt her tipsy glow deepen into a blush. How could she be so naked with a virtual stranger?

"We all want warmth, Mandy," Sam soothed. "You just have to figure out how to get what you need."

"Have you figured that out?"

"As a matter of fact I have." His smile took on a wolfish air. "But I'm not sure a card-carrying feminist like you wants to hear the details."

"I can take anything you dish out. Don't you remember?"

Sam's grin widened and his fingers brushed hers casually, sending a jolt of lust straight to her pussy.

"All right, then, I'll be blunt. I'm not interested in a traditional relationship right now myself, but I always enjoy the company of lovely ladies. So I host sex parties at my house a few times a week. Not on weekends when I have the kids, of course, but my friends are flexible. Sometimes it turns into what you might call an orgy. Tuesdays are lady's night. That's the singular. One lady, several men."

"A gang bang?" Miranda leaned back in her chair and tried to look cool, belying the hot, fluttery feeling between her legs.

Sam wrinkled his nose. "Nothing so vulgar. It's called a *bukkake* party. The custom's imported from Japan, although in our version, the lady always calls the shots, so to speak. It's much more interesting that way."

"What's 'boo-kah-kay'?" Miranda's numb lips struggled to pronounce the strange word.

With a mischievous glint in his eye, Sam proceeded to explain exactly what transpired at his house on Tuesday nights. Apparently, there was a bed with a plastic sheet and something softer to cover it, and the woman knelt or lay down on it. Usually she was naked, but she didn't have to be, and the men lined up around the bed and...

Here Miranda instinctively raised her hand to stop the troubling and oddly arousing image taking shape in her mind. "No woman would ever consent to that."

Sam laughed. "Actually, they volunteer. I have a waiting list for months. But I'd be happy to arrange a special session for you."

"*I* could never do such a thing," she insisted, clutching her cold, slippery glass.

"Miranda, you're a free woman. You can do anything you want. And I can guarantee you'll find plenty to warm you in my humble party room."

That's when he took her hand. His flesh was indeed warm and faintly moist. The sensation was a bit...dirty...and yet her fingers immediately relaxed into the heat.

As if they'd finally found a place to rest.

That's how she came to be here in this strange room, splayed out on his *bukkake* bed for the fourth time in a month. Sam had scheduled a series of Thursday sessions just for her. Each week the number of guests grew.

Miranda heard more male voices passing below the window—*Are you sure they have "events" here? This looks like my mother-in-law's place....*

From the chuckles, Miranda guessed it was a group of four, maybe five. Which meant they would soon be ready to begin.

She positioned her arms at her sides, suppressing a shiver. She would feel nothing for now. She was an object. A fresh canvas. Pure and clean.

And the men, her therapists—Sam was right to call this her "treatment"—they were pure, too. For when is a man ever more honestly himself than the moment when his hot seed shoots out through his cock to find its home?

The voices were inside the house now, moving closer. The guest room door opened.

She heard a soft "Whoa, nice," and a "Pretty tonight."

Miranda's cunt tensed in a spasm so intense she wondered if they could see her muscles jerk through the negligee. She curled her hands around her thighs to steady herself.

The air around the bed grew thick with the rasp of breathing, the mineral scent of trousers, hints of cumin sweat, crotch musk and palpable excitement.

Under the blindfold, the room began to spin.

She sensed a familiar fragrance of woodsy soap moving toward the head of the bed. It was Sam, of course, presiding over the feast like a patriarch at Thanksgiving.

"I'll explain the rules again for the benefit of the newcomers," he began cordially. "No touching unless she requests it, but she likes it when you talk, so say whatever comes into your dirty minds. Don't expect an answer though. She only speaks to command. There are some bottles of lube over there with the tissues if you want it. Oh, and last but not least, we have a big crowd tonight, so watch your aim. I've already gotten this carpet cleaned twice this month."

The air above her crackled with laughter.

"How close can I get?" This voice sounded young, nervous.

"Need practice with that chip shot?"

More laughter.

"Make room for the boy," a deeper voice called and there was shuffling around the bed, then the purr of zippers, the rustle of cloth.

In spite of herself—she was just an object after all—Miranda tilted her head back and sighed.

"She looks good tonight."

"Yeah, nice nightgown. A shame to ruin it."

Ruin. The very sound of the word made her juice up down there like a drooling baby.

"Her tits look bigger today." This voice was Brooklyn. A regular.

"You must have had too many Manhattans. Or maybe you need your reading glasses?"

"Fuck off. Tonight I'm gonna come right in that pretty pink valley."

"But she's already got a pearl necklace," said another, the jocular fellow who was the first to arrive.

"Women always want more jewelry," added a smooth voice. Miranda imagined a silk ascot, an overpriced watch.

That's right. Talk. Talk dirty to me.

Miranda felt the sweat rise on her skin. Blank canvas she might be, but her chest was tingling, aching for touch. She cupped her own breasts and flicked the nipples with her thumbs.

"Fuck, I love to watch them masturbate." That was Brooklyn again, but the words had a tug-tug rhythm, as if his own hand were busy with a similar task.

"That's not masturbation. She's not fingering her cunt."

"She's turning herself on, asshole, that's jerking off."

"This is jerking off," grunted an unfamiliar voice, and before she could brace herself, a burning hot volley of spunk sprayed Miranda's chest from the left, coating her fingers in thick goo.

For a moment the room was completely still.

Miranda almost giggled. This happened every time, the breathless pause after the first man shot his load. What did they expect? Indignation? Surprise? *How ungentlemanly of you to ejaculate on my breasts, sir?*

Surely the veterans knew what came next. That instead of protesting she would lift her dripping hand to her nose and inhale deeply of the very mystery that brought her here—the intoxicating elixir of summer sunshine and new-mown hay. Miranda drew another deep breath, resisting the urge to taste it. With her clean hand, she grabbed the dental dam at her side and waved it in the general direction of the man who'd baptized her.

"You, Mr. Early Bird," she said, assuming the confident V.P.-of-marketing tone that served her so well at the office. "Eat my pussy."

To facilitate her command, she hiked the negligee up over her thighs and spread her legs wide.

Someone whistled.

"Aw, man, I love wet pussy," sighed another.

"Yeah, nice pink twat. You're a lucky man, even if you have to wear a raincoat."

"I thought the winner was the one who held out." That was the youngster.

"We all win," Sam assured him. "You'll see."

Mr. Early Bird was now scooting up between her legs. He had a broad frame and Miranda had to stretch her legs wider to accommodate him. The high slits of the negligee tore farther up toward her waist. She moaned, exhilarated by the sound of heedless destruction, the proof of her descent into pure wantonness.

The man grabbed her heels and placed them on his shoulders. The heat of his body oozed through the soles of her feet, melting her calf and thigh muscles. He began to lick. The latex grew warm. Miranda had come to enjoy this slightly muffled sensation, as if he were pleasuring her through thick cotton panties.

She whimpered and clutched at the sheet.

"What does she want the rest of us to do?" the young man fretted.

"Figuring that out is part of the fun." Sam laughed.

"She wants us to get her very, very messy," explained the jocular guy.

"I've never seen a real woman who enjoys a money shot like she does," agreed the smooth voice.

"Yeah, this one's really into it," said Brooklyn. "Sometimes she shoots her own puddle on the bed as if she's taking notes from us."

Miranda let out a soft "Oh," half in shame—the man was right that she left quite a mess herself—and half in delirium from the overwhelming bounty of attention. So many men were gazing at her, wanting her. Even through the blindfold, she could feel their glowing eyes stroke her skin. Their rude, nasty comments aroused her like perfectly calibrated spankings on her most secret flesh. Nor could she find fault with the agile tongue working her clit through the latex. If she let herself go, she could easily come soon, but she was still too blank, too clean.

"Hey, Early Bird. Stop." The warmth between her thighs receded with a disappointed smack of lips. "Now, whoever jerks off on me before I count to ten takes his place."

Someone snorted a protest, but soon enough the air was alive with new sounds: determined panting, soft moans and the clicking cricketlike song of hands yanking swollen dicks.

Miranda counted out the numbers, her voice unsteady. *One...Two....*

At eight, her left hip was pelted with hot rain. This was immediately followed by a copious eruption that sprayed across the hollow of her rib cage and another shower on her arm and shoulder.

Her body jerked, as if enduring a series of rapid blows.

Fingers plucked another dental dam from her side. "My turn, sweetheart."

"Can I come on her again?" asked the young man.

"Oh, to be twenty-one again," Brooklyn teased.

"Go ahead," Sam said. "She likes it. The more jizz, the better."

The second man was crawling up on the bed now. He tilted her thighs up so that her feet dangled in the air. Stretching the dam tight over her vulva, he went right to work, nipping her clit gently through the thin barrier.

Her belly began to throb, a pulsing nova in her groin. She couldn't hold back much longer. This next part was tricky, but they hadn't let her down yet.

"Come on me," she barked, "Shoot your wad in the next two minutes or you have to take your aching balls back home with you."

"Bossy bitch, isn't she?"

"Better get to work," Sam said cheerfully. "I've got my stopwatch on."

A new voice to Miranda's right gave a grunt, as if he'd been punched. With a growling "Fuck, fuck, fuck," he glazed her right side with spurts of hot cream.

"Watch out, you got me."

"Sorry, man, sorry."

Brooklyn, at her left shoulder, let out a high-pitched yelp and ejaculated over her chest, knocking against the bed rhythmically with each spasm.

"Excuse me, if I may, I've got a present for the lady." The smooth, moneyed voice spoke with uncharacteristic urgency. Within moments new arcs of jism joined the growing deposit on her chest.

"That's seven," Miranda said. "Who's left?"

"I am."

She should have known it would be Sam. Naturally a good host would make sure his guests' needs were satisfied before he claimed his own.

"Come on the pearls. Shoot all over them," she ordered.

The bed lurched. Sam was kneeling over her, his knees pressed against her side. She smelled cock, a hint of soap, the vaguely medicinal scent of lube. Her eyes began to tear with something close to gratitude. The sound of fist pumping cock filled her ears, and she felt her own heartbeat quicken to keep pace with his quick jerks.

Just then Sam cupped her cheek, tenderly, as if he were about to make love to her. "Take this, you greedy, come-covered slut."

His voice was so perversely gentle that what came next actually took her by surprise: one, two, three, four pulsing jets of ejaculate oozing over her collarbone and neck, coating the white beads with warm, sticky glaze.

"Rub it on me, all of you," Miranda cried. She grabbed the sperm-soaked lace and ripped the negligee open over her breasts. "Paint it the fuck all over me."

Dozens of fingers obediently scooped up the viscous cream and began to massage her, anointing her nipples with it, icing her belly. Wherever they rubbed, her nerves sprang to life. One hand soothed the spunk from her neck over her shoulders, which were suddenly as exquisitely sensitive as a clit. Others spread gobs of it over her breasts, massaging her, healing her with the smooth, silky ointment.

"God, oh, god, yes," she cooed, wanting them all to see how much she loved this. So many men were disgusted by their own come, but for her, at this moment, it was an intimate gift, the most honest exchange possible between a man and a woman. It wasn't pretty, but she was done with pretty—pearls and satin, vows of eternal love and all those other lies that only made her feel dirtier in the end.

Desperately, she pressed her cunt up against the tireless tongue still brushing and stroking her swollen clit. It was her turn to give them a gift, to let them see a come-covered slut abandon herself to the ultimate animal release. Her mouth twisted into a grimace.

I'm going to come, oh, god...

Damn if she wasn't doing it, too, coming, thrashing, screaming, gushing all over the sheet as eight faceless men urged her on with their slippery caresses.

She collapsed back onto the bed, limp, drenched, released.

"Nice show."

"Yeah, that was wild."

"Thanks, sweetheart. I'll be sure to come again next week."

Only then did she grace them with a smile.

"Well, it's time to retire for our port and cigars, gentlemen," Sam announced.

"The bathroom's the second door on the left if you'd like to wash up."

Miranda lay still until the men filed out and the door closed firmly behind them. Then she sat up and pulled off the blindfold to survey the damage. The negligee was a mess—stained, torn, stinking of locker room and spunk. Grinning, she peeled it from her body and stuffed it in the plastic-lined trash can beside the bed. Next she unclasped the goo-covered pearls and dropped them onto the crumpled gown.

"Goodbye, Tom," she whispered.

Stepping into the guest bathroom, she washed her hands under hot water and dried them with one of the soft towels stacked neatly on the counter. Her chest still tingled, and she touched it with her heat-flushed fingertips. The skin was tender yet stronger, like a scar. Spunk really did seem to nourish her. She would sleep well tonight.

As for Sam's standing invitation, Miranda felt no desire for him now. She would slip out the back, as usual, and be on her way. One day, when the lingerie drawer was empty and her jewelry box bare, she might stay. Until then she was far too greedy for one man to satisfy.

Before her shower, she paused for one last look at herself. The woman in the mirror over the sink made quite a painting, the dried semen decorating her chest and neck like fine lace. But this was no hesitant nymph, no wistful modernist muse. She was a Titian duchess, patron of the arts, a woman who could commission her own portrait that glowed with radiance beyond any commonplace beauty or understanding.

Miranda straightened her shoulders and lifted her chin high. After these Thursday night treatments, this formidable lady with her sly, satisfied expression was no stranger.

The woman smiling back at her seemed to agree.

TWO COCKS, ONE GIRL

Cecilia Tan

When my boyfriend became obsessed with other men's cocks, I knew my life was going to change. The names have been changed in this story to reflect how absurd it is, so let's call my boyfriend "Peter." See, thing is, it was high time for a change, anyway. Peter was working a kind of crap job doing phone support for low pay, and I hadn't had a job in two years, but that's the recessionary economy. We were still pretty happy, not living large, but being good to each other and still having regular sex even after ten years together.

The first time I noticed Peter getting interested in other guys' junk was when we were watching porn. A typical Friday night for us, if we didn't have our gaming group over, was we'd download whatever we could get and then lie in bed watching it on one of our laptops until we got so horny we couldn't stand it anymore, and then he'd just fuck my soaked pussy until I came. When you've been together as long as we have, all the other foreplay stuff gets boring, you know? It's as if the only reason we did all the smooching and cuddling and petting back when we were shy virgins was we were too shy to just get right to it. Basically, if I'm wet, I'm good to go. (Plus, there is always lube.)

But we were talking about porn. And my boyfriend. And other men's cocks. Most straight porn is focused on the big-busted babe, but the scenes I like best are the ones where you can't see the faces of the actors, just the penetration. We tried watching animated porn once, but it didn't do much for either of us. We both wanted to see a real cock in action or it seemed sort of pointless. This is why "reality" porn worked just fine for us. Who cares about the bad acting and dumb dialogue in porn movies? What we get off on is watching two real live humans fucking.

Peter started to make comments while we were watching, like, "Do you think that guy's arm gets tired when he jerks off?" and, "I hear they like to hire short actors with big cocks so that their cocks will look even bigger." I would just murmur agreement, maybe stroking his own schlong while we watched. But I noticed a pattern in the films he was downloading. We were seeing more and more of the *Long Dong Silver* and *Freakishly Big Dicks In Action* type of films.

All I can say is there are some amazing specimens of humanity out there. You figure if a guy has a cock that hangs almost to his knees, in the back of his head he's wondering if he might be able to make a good living from his asset, no? Other guys must notice it at the beach and in the gym, right? How hard is it to get an audition with a porn studio, I wonder? Do the actresses get paid more to do scenes with them? In my head I imagined a pay scale based on the inches, or maybe the volume, like stunt men getting paid more for the more dangerous stunts.

Yes, these are the things that went through my head while watching a woman who looked like a ballerina with beach balls on her chest take a schlong the size of a Genoa salami between the legs. And yes, it made me hot—and curious. The next day, while Peter was at work, I started researching pay scales in porn films. I wasn't surprised to learn that the women get paid more than the men, and that a woman who will do anal sex gets more than a woman who won't.

Then Peter started downloading gay porn. The first one was supposedly an "accident." You know, he pulled it off a torrent site and didn't know what it was, but once we started watching it we noticed two things. First off, the guys are actually good-looking, and secondly, there are double the number of cocks. Score! Neither of us missed the beach-ball-busted babes, and the ass was as good as the pussy for those close-up penetration shots.

But it got really serious the night we were watching one of these gay videos that had a kind of rapey theme; you know, where the one guy is reluctant and the other one isn't? The whole thing was in Hungarian so it was hard to figure out exactly what was going on, but the one guy lay the other one down and then rubbed his cock all over the other guy's cock, like giving him a hand job, only it was a cock job.

Peter was tugging on his own salami while we were watching this scene, and he came without warning. He sounded pretty surprised himself, a kind of wordless jumble coming out of his mouth like, "Whu-gub-bahhh-uhhh?" as he shot all over his stomach. I was kind of not pleased with that, since I had been getting close to putting the laptop down at that point, but it was so damn funny at the same time I just ended up laughing. And besides, it didn't even take an hour for him to get it up again.

While we were fucking, I asked, "If I had a cock, would you want me to rub you off with it until you came?"

"Fuck, yeah," he said, but while we're fucking is a totally

unfair time for me to ask him questions, because so often that tends to be the answer. You know, like, "Hey, will you rake the leaves in the back tomorrow?"

"Mm, fuck, yeah..."

So I had to ask him again a couple of days later, when we weren't horny, to see what he'd say. We were making dinner at the time. "Do you want me to get a strap-on?" I asked.

"A what?" It took him a minute to get what I'd said out of context. "Oh, you mean like a dildo?"

"Yeah. You know, so we can try the cock-to-cock thing."

"Oh." He stopped stirring the sauteing onions for a moment while he thought about it. "Eh, I'm not sure. It's like the animation thing."

"You want a Hundred-Percent-Real Cock™, is that it?" I teased.

"Er, well, um." He blushed and the onions began to caramelize. "Don't you think that's kind of too gay for me?"

Peter and I have been together more than ten years. When we first met I'd thought he might be bi and in denial. Ten years later...I was sure of it. But you know how skittish guys can be. Now, I could have just said, "But it turns you on. What's wrong with that?" Or, "There's no such thing as too gay or too straight." Or, "I think having lived with your girlfriend for a decade has kind of saved up your 'nongay' points."

But I didn't. What I said was, "Is it gay if it's a threesome? You know, a girl sandwich?" I reached over and took gentle hold of his wrist at the same time, moving it in a circle so that he'd keep stirring.

"Hm, no, I guess not," he said.

We didn't wait for Friday. That night we downloaded a two-guys-one-girl video.

The following week, I charged a dildo on the one credit card

I had that wasn't maxed out, and started playing with it while Peter was at work. In particular I started using it on my ass. That almost derailed the whole experiment right there because, holy crap, why didn't anyone tell me what an intense orgasm can be had from anal penetration? I guess I figured those porn girls were just faking it so they could get the higher pay. Wrong. But instead of telling Peter we should switch to anal sex, I stuck to the plan, and the next time we had sex, I put the dildo into my ass while Peter was fucking me....

It wasn't an instant orgasm for both of us, but it was pretty damn close.

So this was how the following Friday we ended up canceling our gaming group to meet a guy we had found through Craigslist. Let's call the guy "Dick." The phone conversation went something like this:

Peter: Yeah, so, hi, I thought we should talk about getting together.

Dick: A threesome right? You and your girlfriend? How long you been together?

Peter: Ten years. Actually, this is kind of almost our anniversary.

Me (in the background, with my hand over the phone): Why are you telling him that?

Dick: No kidding? That's cool. I'm like, not looking for a relationship myself right now.

Peter: That's okay. We're not like trying to form a group marriage or something. Just a fun fling, you know?

Dick: So long as we're using condoms, I'm good with it.

Peter: Of course. I wouldn't let you assfuck her without one.

Dick: Is she the only one getting assfucked?

Peter: Yeah.

Dick: That's cool. You want to meet me at a hotel I know? No muss, no fuss.

So we went to this hotel, pretty nice place actually, since I was all for not having to wash the sheets, and if the guy didn't actually come to our place I felt like we were less likely to get cased for a robbery or something. We went up to the room, and Dick had a case of beer and some snacks laid out on the dresser. He was a looker—crew cut, big biceps and a big bulge in his jeans.

He sat on the edge of the bed and leaned back in what I think was supposed to be an alluring pose and asked, "So what do you folks like to do to get in the mood?"

"Oh," I said right away. "We watch porn."

"Awesome." The next thing I knew, we had an adult film playing on the TV, and I had a guy on either side of me sucking on my nipples. Okay, so maybe all foreplay isn't pointless. Plus, it was a threesome flick, so it was very easy when it got to a position that looked doable for me to say, "That. I want to do that."

Dick coaxed Peter to the edge of the bed so that his feet were on the floor and then invited me to hop on. I straddled Peter. I should mention at this point, because he'll be cranky if I don't, that Peter has a big one. And it always feels bigger to me when I'm on top.

Peter said, "Fuck, yeah."

Dick came around the back then, telling Peter to spread his legs apart more, which made my ass nice and inviting. Dick lubed up my ass then and finger-fucked me for a while, and Peter groaned. Later he told me it was like the guy was running his finger up and down Peter's cock…but inside me.

I told him when I thought I was ready. Dick was bigger than the dildo I'd been using, but I was so horny by that point I didn't think it would matter. And ultimately, it didn't, though when he put those first couple of inches in I nearly told him to take it out again and forget the whole plan. But then I felt Peter inside me literally twitching, and...

Fuck, yeah.

It took a little time, but once Dick got all the way in and started a long, slow fuck, I was pretty much in heaven. Peter didn't really have to move, just stay where he was, filling me up. He wasn't wearing a condom; we haven't bothered with those between us since before we moved in together and I got an implant. Dick slid in and out, in and out, getting gradually faster.

"Can you really come just from assfucking?" Dick asked at one point, though because he was nibbling on my sweaty shoulder at the time it came out more like, "Kenya Regal Clone Justice Assfucking?"

I opened my mouth but Peter interrupted, "Holy shit, slow down or you're going to make me come first."

"No! Don't you dare," I said, clawing at Peter's collarbone.

"Trying..." he whined.

"Gotcha," Dick said. "Slower. That's cool."

So it was like a game: could Dick fuck me hard enough to make me come without setting Peter off too soon? I got closer and closer; Peter got closer and closer. Dick wasn't letting on how close he was, but he seemed to have it under control. Very fine control. He and Peter made eye contact over my shoulder, and the next thing I knew it was like they were doing some kind of male-bonding mind-reading thing, speaking only in little grunts and whimpers.

I have no idea how long this went on. The movie we'd loaded up on-demand had ended a while ago. Then Dick got a bright idea. "Would you mind a reach around?"

For a moment I didn't get what he said, but then I felt his fingers slipping over my swollen clit. No, I didn't mind, but what came out was, "Yes, oh, yes," and I guess it was clear I meant "Yes, that's good," because he kept on doing it. He had my clit between two fingers, and every time he pushed into me from behind, my clit was pushed into them. Kind of like a little tiny cock fucking a small pair of legs...

That was the thought that sent me over the edge. And once I went over the edge, Dick didn't hold back, fucking me like a train piston and setting Peter to screaming he was coming so hard. Dick didn't take long either, and it was like I was coming the whole time he was still fucking hard, only waning off as he softened and they both shrank out of me.

Dick took the first shower while Peter and I lay in a sweaty heap on the bed. "That was fucking amazing," I said. "But seriously, was it too gay for you?"

"No," Peter said. "It was awesome." Then he fell asleep, so that was the totality of our processing on that for a while. We went back to just having sex like before after that, but kept up with watching the threesome videos, eventually talking about how we couldn't drag someone else in every week without it getting weird. Maybe for special occasions, you know? Not that we could do much for our actual anniversary when it came, since we were so broke.

But I said it was all going to change, right? The next thing we got into watching was "security camera" sex videos. Now, you can be sure most of the ones you see on the Internet are fake, right? I mean, sometimes they even zoom in and stuff, which a real, static camera wouldn't do. Also the sites have these disclaimers about all models being over eighteen, which kind of killed the idea for me that there could be real unwitting participants in it.

That is, until I found us. The description was something like, "Brunette vixen gets DP'd by nerd and hunk in hotel room." Okay, yeah, Peter is a nerd, but I didn't even think of us until the video actually started playing, and then it became obvious there had been a camera in the set-top box. Yeah, I know, I should have been outraged.

But damn, that night was the best sex Peter and I had since the night of the threesome itself.

While we were lying in an exhausted pile afterward I got to thinking, and, well, once I'd put it all together, it really wasn't that hard to get started. Peter and I own a couple of websites now, including Threesomes-R-Us.com, Girl-Sandwich.com, and Two-Cocks-One-Girl.com. We haven't even made that many videos and we don't have to, because people keep coming and watching the ones that are there for money, plus there's ad revenue. Peter is still in denial about being bi, but still gets off on the sensation of another man's cock on his, as long as it's inside my body. That's all right. I'm the boss now, and he's happy. I hire the guys who do it with us for the shoots.

I pay them by the inch.

SKINHEADS

Jacqueline Applebee

I was only a little girl when I started following the fascists home. I didn't know what that word meant back then; I just knew that's what people called the gang of skinhead white boys who walked through Belmont Park, scattering all in their path. I guess it was the power they seemed to radiate that snared me: the lean but muscular legs and arms, the arrogant, sneering faces. I loved the way they used to stare at people, intimidating anyone who came close.

North London in the 1970s was not the healthiest place to be a black child. At that age I never appreciated the danger I put myself in every day after school. I didn't know the white boys I was attracted to hated people like me. In fact they hated just about anyone who wasn't like them. I only knew that my first stirring of desire for the opposite sex sparked at the exact same time when most boys at school wore the worst fashions ever seen. I was surrounded by swathes of beige nylon trousers, polyester shirts and stripy school ties. The skinheads dressed differently. They wore tight white shirts, tighter washed-out denim jeans held up by black braces. But the thing that got me scurrying around behind them, when sense told me to stop, was the boots. Pairs of brightly polished Doc Martens would stomp ahead of me, disappearing out of sight to where my little brown legs could not follow. Ever since then, I've hankered after boots with at least fifteen holes.

I heard things. I saw the bruises, the smudges of red over fists. People told me to stay away from them; teachers grew concerned that I would try to exact some kind of childish revenge for the way the white boys treated the black ones. I was a tiny girl. What could I do? Besides, the way the skinheads treated the black boys was no different from how the black boys treated most black girls.

As an adult I still found myself craving skinheads. I'm no longer a little girl—even barefoot, I'm as tall as most guys I know. I soon discovered gay men who wore outfits identical to those that the fascists sported back in North London. I saw people reclaim the look, the tight lines, the shaven heads and the tattoos. But to me, it was always about the white boys strutting around as if they owned the whole bloody world.

My desire led me to Camden, to a warehouse where I had arranged to meet a friend of a friend, called Stuart. I was also to meet his "boy," which was the real reason I was hanging around with the tramps and tourists on a hot Saturday afternoon.

Stuart, a tall solid man, met me by the stairs as I sheltered in what little shade I could find. He wore a black leather kilt, and boots the color of blood. He looked me up and down before he held out his hand. I gave him the agreed upon money—a clutch of notes in an envelope that he counted quickly in the shadow of the stairs.

He turned to me, speaking in a low voice. "I'll not have my boy marked in any way."

I sighed. "Is this little talk necessary?"

"I know what you women are like with all that cutting business."

"I've got no interest in that."

Stuart looked at me a moment longer before he inclined his head. I followed him. I could see up his kilt as he walked ahead of me, but it was his boots that held my attention.

Stuart's boy stood in a corner of a large dusty room. He looked nervous. Like Stuart, he was tall with a shaven head; in his early twenties, I assumed. But unlike Stuart, this boy wore bleached denim trousers that stretched tight over his thighs. Stress lines in the fabric crossed this way and that.

"He'll do just fine." I put my large bag down.

"I'll be over here if you need me." Stuart pointed to a single chair against the wall near the door.

"You're staying?" That wasn't part of the agreement. I blew out an annoyed puff of air. I wasn't going to start arguing about it now. "He got a name?"

"I'm Darren." Stuart's boy looked less nervous now, more pissed-off at being addressed like that by a black woman.

I smiled, took a step closer to the young man. He swallowed, looked away for a moment. I ran a hand over his thin belt; I would have preferred him to wear braces, but it would have to do. I hooked my fingers around the leather, pulled him to me. Darren grunted, but said nothing. I held his hand, pressed it to my jeans, to where the harness I wore beneath sat snug against my skin. I knew he could feel the buckles and rings when he smirked at me.

"Are you one of them chicks with dicks?"

He barely said the words before I smacked him hard across the mouth. "Excuse me?" I asked politely.

"Shit!" Darren touched his lip, which was already starting to swell.

I raised my hand once more. Darren flinched, looked to the corner where Stuart was. I felt a stir behind me, saw a shadow move on the dusty floor, but it retreated after a moment. I'd learnt this little dance from years of watching older boys intimidate younger ones. I'd memorized the way that force could be used—not in excess, so as to attract unwanted attention, but just enough to get your point across.

"Take them off." I stroked down his torso for a brief moment before I stepped away. I watched as Darren peeled off his tight top.

All the times I risked life and limb by creeping into the boys' changing rooms at school had finally paid off. I was no longer a little girl peeking around corners to see glimpses of flesh. Today, I was getting the whole damn show.

Darren had a smattering of hair over his tiny nipples. Blond wisps collected in a line down the center of his stomach, down to the tops of his pants where it got darker. He reached for the laces on his boots.

"Keep those on."

"I can't get my pants off if I keep them on," he complained.

"Do yer best, Darren," Stuart called out. I could have done without his input. I wanted the boy to concentrate on me, not his old man.

I unzipped my jeans and then bent to my bag where my black dildo lay among a variety of toys and tools. It only took a moment to fasten it to the harness I wore.

Darren took several steps away when he caught sight of my silicone erection. "You're never going to put that thing in me!"

I heard Stuart sigh, along with the scrape of his chair on the hard floor. He stood beside me, peering down at my dick. "I've seen bigger," he smirked. I gave him a look and put my hands on my hips. Stuart raised his hands, stepped away.

I returned to Darren, who was now pouting. I slid his belt out of its loops. He wriggled, looking uncomfortable, embarrassed. I wasn't about to make things any easier for him. When I shook my head, he visibly drew himself up to his full height, puffed out his chest. It took all my concentration to not laugh at the spectacle.

"Bitch, please," I said with a smirk.

"She called me a bitch!" Darren squeaked in complaint, looking in Stuart's direction.

"Must I put up with this?" I asked out loud. "Do I have to request a refund?"

Darren stilled. His hands returned to his pants, which he pushed down with effort until they lay bunched around his knees. Even with the drama-queen attitude, he was still my living, breathing, wet dream.

"I think I'll take you up against the wall."

Darren shuffled to the nearest wall, his clumsy movements disturbing the dust into little blooms. I followed him, fingering the dildo I wore. I rolled a condom over my silicone length. I could feel the lines of sensation travel up my body from my clit to my breasts, electricity that was so intense and sharp, it was physically painful. However, I tended to enjoy pain—whether giving or receiving, I always lapped it up.

When I reached the boy, I was buzzing, burning up with anticipation and need. I braced my hands on either side of his head and rubbed myself over his back, over his bare arse that had a little tattoo on it: a St. Andrew's flag. I lost myself in simply feeling his hot body beneath me. My dildo prodded his thighs, the curve of his arsecheeks.

"I'm ready," Darren said.

"I'm sure you think you are." I stretched around to his front, felt the hot burn of his erection on my palm.

"Go on then, do it," he hissed. "Just do it."

My little bottle of lube sat in my back pocket. I applied a liberal amount to my fingers and then pushed one between his cheeks. I circled around, enjoying the sight of him writhing against the wall. I stepped back slightly, and then with my free hand I slapped his arse, making him jump with surprise. I spanked him some more, steady beats that turned his white-boy skin a rosy red. When I returned my hand to his cock, it felt harder, hotter.

"Now you're ready."

Darren whimpered. The sound of surrender made my nipples tingle. I wanted to hear him make more noises like that.

The first slide of my cock into his body was a sucking squelch. I breathed out along Darren's neck, exhaling the stored-up passion and want that had stirred inside me all those years ago. I pushed farther, implanting myself inside the boy. My feet were unsteady. My hips moved of their own accord. My head spun. He didn't have to do a thing to surrender his power. It leapt off his skin, dribbled with the sweat that ran down his back. I licked around his throat, pressing teeth to the flesh that was stretched tight. I wrapped my arms around him, possessively circled his body with mine.

"Please," he whispered into the wall. He arched up against me. I understood of course. I had power of my own. I brought down my hand against his arse once more. He shuddered beneath me, bucking slightly as I slapped him again and again.

A movement to my left made me look up, gasping, into the eyes of Stuart. His kilt was held up by a large pin. He grabbed his cock in his fist, stroking it hard and fast. He nodded at me. Knowledge and power combined into a potent aphrodisiac as I mirrored his movements with my own. I circled my hand around the boy's cock, pulling and stroking in the same way that

Stuart touched himself. Darren leant back against me, his weight threatening to push me over. I pressed him back against the wall fully, continued to jerk him off as I thrust inside.

"Shit!"

I don't know which of the men swore out loud, but warm come erupted over my hand a moment after. Stuart squeezed his eyes shut, and then he came too, spraying his boy with thick streaks of white.

I breathed deep. My clitoris sung with pleasure, even though I hadn't come yet. That was something I'd do later when I was alone at home. My orgasm was a powerful moment that I wasn't about to let these guys see.

I slid out of Darren's arse carefully. He winced and squeaked with every movement until I was free of him. He sagged against the dusty wall, sticky and sweaty. He didn't look so tough now, although his boots were still impressive. I pulled the spent condom from my dildo, threw it down on the dirty floor. I felt my own power surge within at what I'd done. Somewhere inside me, a little girl jumped for joy.

"Will you be wanting to make this a regular arrangement?" Stuart's voice was raspy, breathless.

"Make him wear braces next time. I don't want to see the belt again." I sounded hoarse, too.

"Yes, ma'am," Stuart said, with a smile. "That's not a problem at all."

I straightened myself out, picked up my bag and left without another word. But as I descended the metal stairs and strode out into the bustle of Camden on a busy afternoon, I felt like I owned the whole bloody world.

KING SLUT

Valerie Alexander

Scene I

The actor playing the king stands against a backdrop of palm trees, his sandaled feet motionless on a three-foot dais. His muscled arms are a golden bronze, his chiseled chest and abs taut. He wears only a kilt of white linen, banded just beneath his narrow hips, with gold snake bracelets twining round his biceps. In one hand he grips a staff. But his face is concealed beneath a golden King Tut mask, its famous noble face staring past the director, cameramen and waiting extras with the poise of a real pharaoh.

"This isn't at all true to life," says one of the grips. "That mask was a death mask they found in his sarcophagus. Tutankhamen never wore it in real life."

"We're shooting a porn movie called King Slut,*" the director says. "You really think anybody gives a shit?"*

A female PA says, "I think the mask is hot. Without it, he's just another guy."

"I'm sure our star really appreciates that," the director says. "Come on now. Back to work."

King Slut stands motionless on the dais as if deaf to their words.

Cecilia pauses the porn movie running in her head. It's her own creation and she can return to it later, even if she'd prefer to be watching it right now instead of the movie currently broadcasting before her. But she has to be social. She's at a party; next to her is her fiercest crush, and he and the sixteen other people here are silently absorbed in their hostess's art-porn project, which Cecilia pretends to like to be polite. The film isn't working for her, though. She knows it's supposed to be better than typical porn fare, the kind with a lot of bleached hair, fake moans and mechanical fucking, because it's shot in black and white and the actresses are just local art student goth girls. But watching the girls finger themselves and stare moodily into the camera leaves Cecilia cold. She looks around at the other guests, their faces rapt in the flickering light and feels like a freak. Even watching cable soft-core porn with her friend Shea is better than this, because they snark and make up fake dialogue for the actors.

She sneaks a look at Adam next to her. His hazel eyes look pensive, the profile of his full lips and sculpted cheekbones making her heart give a little jump. She's wanted him for so long, obsessing over his remote beauty, his maddening aloofness, and now here he is at last. She can tell he's hers if she wants him. He devoted enough time to her last weekend at a different party to convey that. But his absorption in the film makes her wonder how sexually predictable he is. He's so quiet, it's hard to read him.

She gets up and goes into the kitchen to find another beer.

He comes after her and leans up against the counter, bracing his foot against a cabinet. "You seem kind of fidgety."

She opens the beer. "The movie's kind of boring."

He laughs awkwardly. "Okay... So what would entertain you?"

She takes a long swallow of the beer and puts it on the counter without taking her eyes off his.

Now Adam looks surprised—but then he shakes back his long, dark hair with a studied cool, takes her hand and leads her outside. The backyard is bluish with moonlight. They look around—the ground is muddy and scattered with fallen leaves and looks cold—then at each other. And then he's touching her, his hands sliding up her sides, his mouth hot on hers in the cold night. She feels something open up in her and swoon. A moment later they're on the patio, the cold concrete going through her shirt as she hooks her legs around his. His cock is hard and pressing through his jeans.

She rubs her pussy up against him just before the back door bangs open, followed by a giggle.

"Oh...sorry, Cecilia. But we're leaving." It's her best friend, Shea.

Adam pulls her to her feet and helps her brush off her jeans. "I can give you a ride," he says with a loaded look.

It would be so easy to go home with him. She's wanted it for months. Instead she declines. "No, I really should go. Sorry."

On the way home, Shea expresses her approval. "Making him work for it, I like it," she says. "I notice that Amy's film got you all excited, though. You two were the first ones to go off together."

"Ugh, the film. Don't tell Amy, but I hated it."

Shea is surprised. "You didn't like it? Why not?"

"Did you not notice the complete lack of penis in it? I'm

straight, Amy's straight, why can't we have a movie with some
boys in it? Why do I have to look at naked girls all the time?"

Shea seems taken aback. "Well, you didn't like the guys in
that pirate porn movie we saw."

Cecilia thinks of the pirate movie actors: stone-faced, not
sexy or even good-looking really, and they'd fucked the actresses
likes robots. But before she can say that, Shea says, "I guess
you're just not the porn type."

Cecilia is half tempted to tell Shea about her *King Slut* movie.
*Actually, Shea, I have my own mental porn; it's based on this
weird King Tut fixation I have. I even got a copy of that famous
mask at a Halloween store. You probably didn't notice but
Adam sort of looks like an Egyptian pharaoh...*

But she's too embarrassed. As sexual fixations go, it's hardly
something she can explain. King Tut's golden death mask capti-
vated her as soon as she saw it in her college archeology class.
The exotic cheekbones; the kohl-lined, almond-shaped eyes: it
seemed like the most sensual, perfect face in the world. That the
king had died at eighteen only made him more fascinating. She
looked up everything she could find about him and sometimes,
when she had sex, she would try to visualize the man beneath
her wearing that famous mask. She didn't tell anyone as her
fantasies expanded into her ongoing and elaborate *King Slut*
mind-movie. Only when she found the mask in the Halloween
store last year, did she entertain the thought of making it reality;
of finding the right man to wear it while fucking her senseless.

Scene II
*"Let's move on, people. King, you're going fowl-hunting up the
Nile. Three slave girls in the boat. Take one."*

*King Slut emerges from his dressing room in costume. No
one can tell what he's really thinking because of the mask but his*

white kilt is down: no wood. Everyone watches his hard thigh muscles roll as he moves to the river and waiting canoe. Production has done a good job of supplying realistic reeds.

The three waiting slave girls are very pretty in black, fringed wings. There was some discussion about them starting out topless but it was finally agreed that it was hotter to have them stripped on board. All of them wear snowy white short linen dresses. A servant extra extends his long pole into the river and they're off.

The sun is shining. King Slut reclines on his elbows, thighs spread comfortably, his biceps bulging. The mask seems to be smiling as he surveys the Nile. Before him the slave girls giggle and whisper, trying to out-cute each other for his attention. The reeds stir with birds. He leaps to attention, javelin in hand. His long bronzed back is motionless, his lateral muscles posed for throwing.

Then a slave girl shoves another girl into him, knocking him off course and startling the birds, who fly away.

"You stupid girl!" the servant roars. "How dare you interfere with the king's hunt! You must take your punishment."

The girl falls to her knees before him, crying. Without a word, King Slut lifts her up by the arm, turns her around, then lightly shoves her so she topples over his footstool. He throws her white dress up, exposing her pussy to everyone on the boat. She trembles, face red, but he has no mercy; he nudges her feet apart until her legs are spread wide open.

The king spanks her with the javelin, slow, measured blows that lay down red marks on the firm smoothness of her ass. She cries harder and wiggles against the stool, but everyone can see she is rubbing her clit against the cushion. As her sobs turn to moans, the young king's kilt begins to protrude.

He rips it off and for the first time in production, shows his cock to the cast and crew. It's long and thick, as rumored. A low, collective sigh fills the room. It slaps his tight stomach as he lifts the slave girl up by the hips and positions her pussy at the tip of his shaft. From this angle, her slit looks too small to take it. He bumps his engorged head against her and makes her moan without really penetrating her.

The servant hisses an order. One of the remaining slave girls quickly pulls off her dress and squats naked behind the king. She strokes his thighs before inserting her tongue between his asscheeks. The other slave girl takes her place before the girl being punished and pulls up her dress with a smirk.

The king pushes abruptly into the first girl. She cries out, with pain or excitement it's impossible to tell and grips the stool for balance as he begins to saw his beautiful cock in and out of her tight little cunt. She's moaning now, her breasts bouncing over the stool, but her moans go muffled when her head is lifted by the hair and pressed against the other slave girl's pussy.

The king's ass squeezes in time with his thrusts. His mask barely moves as he fucks her; he is a strong, taut machine of pelvic action. Only a trickle of sweat dividing his pecs hints at his efforts.

The two other slave girls abandon their positions and bend over before him. He fucks them all, one after another, holding their hips and driving into them like a rocket, making them squeal and bounce for real. This isn't acting. The girls are coming, coming in wet, gasping little throbs from the glory of that huge royal cock fucking them into oblivion.

The crew is barely breathing. King Slut at last pulls out and strokes his cock until he comes all over his own godlike chest. The slave girls eagerly lick it off his muscles like hungry kittens.

"Cut," says the director.

* * *

On a rainy Thursday afternoon, Cecilia goes downtown to the sushi restaurant where Adam is a server. It's almost three and she's hoping the hour, the lull between lunch and dinner, will mean the restaurant is empty and she can have Adam's attention to herself. But it's packed. She can only get a seat at the sushi bar, not a table in his section, and she feels like a stalker as she stares at the menu.

"Holy shit, it's you."

Adam looks so pleased. She puts down the menu and tries to smile. "Sorry about leaving so early the other night. Shea was my ride..."

"I told you I would have given you a ride."

"I know. You did say that." She's starting to feel flustered. "Are you my server?"

"No, but hang on. I'll be back."

In fact, they barely get a chance to speak until she's done eating. She writes her phone number on a napkin but before she can give it to him, he's at her side holding out a receipt with his own number. "Maybe we can get a drink this weekend," he says.

Too easy, she thinks as she heads home. But, of course, the awkward part is still ahead of her. She keeps replaying the predictability of their make-out session on the patio last weekend; you put your hand here, I put my mouth there, as choreographed as a dance routine. That isn't what she wants. Adam looks so perfect for what she does want, that she's half afraid to test him. If he says no, or worse, if they try this and fail, it could debilitate her *King Slut* movie permanently. She thinks about the men who've bragged to her about being able to last for an hour, about her ex who kept bringing home porn for her featuring actors with the biggest cocks in the business. She'd never been able to explain to any of them the weirdness of her orgasm theater. But she wants Adam enough to try.

Scene III
"Okay, people, let's get it together," the director says. "This is the scene where King Slut and Ankhesenamen get together. It's a chariot race, and they're touching each other for the first time. So let's bring that to the scene, okay? Everyone in position."

It's a difficult scene to shoot. The king is taking out his best horse to impress his future wife, Princess Ankhesenamen. The princess is very young and quite shy, clutching her white dress to her thighs as they fly across the plains. Her dark doe eyes are wide with excitement and fear, the blue faience beads in her hair clicking wildly as the king drives the chariot faster. He is a glory to behold, attuned with his horse to the point of communion. But today the princess's hands clutching his sides distract him. Her soft pelvis rattles against him, making his cock rigid.

He leans against the wood, trying desperately to satisfy himself this way. But he wants her. He makes the horse change direction, forcing Princess Ankhesenamen to slide her arms around his waist and hold him tight. Her breasts against his back drive him crazy. Abandoning royal decorum, he takes her small hand and wraps it around his cock.

Shocked at first, the princess begins to tentatively play with his shaft. The king holds his breath. Her touch is too delicate. He puts his hand over hers and shows her how to do it, how to squeeze him, stroke him.

The race is a distant roar. He brings the chariot to a stop, turns around and pushes her against the wood. He pulls off her dress so fast the princess is naked before she can stop him. A faint protest of fear escapes her but when he orders her to spread her legs, she obeys. The king runs his hand between her thighs, *playing with her cunt until she bites her lip. He smiles and slips one finger deep into her heat. She is soaking. But he doesn't fuck her. Instead he slowly rubs the inside of her cunt, tickling her clit with his other hand until she moans and desperately rides against his fingers.*

"Cut."

"So," says Adam. "Here we are."

He's sitting stiffly on her couch, looking nervous. He looks incredible, actually, in a black T-shirt that suits his coloring, and she likes that he's taken pains to look good for her. But the way she asked him to come over instead of going out for drinks seems to have knocked him off his game.

"Indeed." She hands him his drink. In her head, this all went so smoothly. But now that he's actually in her apartment, somehow taller and more vivid than she remembered, she can't remember the words she'd planned to use.

"Nice place." He's said that once already. He looks around her living room until his gaze alights on a framed photo of her and Shea dressed up as zombies last Halloween. "Is that you?"

"In the rotting flesh."

He leans over to look closely at it. "I thought girls always tried to look sexy on Halloween."

"Eh. I think it's the men who should dress sexy for us." Now she sees her opening.

He gives her an odd look. "But women are the ones with all the sex costumes. Naughty nurses, cat girls, belly dancers... What do men have?"

"Well, you have to be creative." Her mouth is so dry. "Like, dressing up as an Egyptian pharaoh would be hot. I even have the King Tut mask."

He stares at her without expression. It reminds her of the first time she saw him, how remote and unattainable he seemed.

"Really?" he says finally. "That, uh, that famous gold mask? I think it's a death mask?"

"That's the one." Her face is getting hot so she adds quickly, "I bought it for my ex-boyfriend but he didn't want to wear it."

He smiles. "And you actually think that's a turn-on?"

"Well, yeah. I've always wanted someone to dress up like a pharaoh for me. It's kind of weird, I know."

They look at each other without comment. Her heart is booming. Then Adam takes a long drink, brushes his hands on his jeans and stands up. The silence is excruciatingly loud and she wishes she had put on some music.

"So what's the rest of the costume?" he asks. "Like a breastplate or something?"

"There isn't one. Just the mask."

Without smiling, he says, "Well, then, I guess I'll have to be naked."

He pulls off his T-shirt. His nipples are hard and dark rose, his stomach tight. She can barely breathe as he unzips his jeans and slides them off along with his underwear. And then he's finally naked, his cock already hard and flushed dark with blood.

His lips jerk in the imitation of a smile. But his thighs are shaking and she can tell he's as nervous as she is.

She stands up. "You are perfect," she tells him and leads him to her bedroom. Smoothing his black hair behind his ears, she puts the mask over his head.

It's really happening. The sex god of her fantasies is going to be possessed and fucked and known totally. He acquiesces silently as she handcuffs him to her bed frame, then plays with his cock until he groans. She squeezes his ass, bites his nipples, a little delirious with the smell and taste of him. Cupping his balls, she tests the weight of them, then runs one fingertip around his asshole. He seems to understand that she doesn't want him to speak. Instead he arches his back against the bed frame and opens his legs, wordlessly beseeching her to tend to his cock.

Cecilia wants to climb on top of him. Instead she slips off the bed and gets her camera. "Keep your legs open," she orders. She starts taking pictures of him, as if to retain proof of this chimera made flesh. "Scoot toward me, until you're really pulling against the cuffs. Good.."

Just looking at him makes her pussy ache. King Slut is handcuffed naked to her bed, yet it's Adam too, and the reality that she's going to fuck them both at the same time makes her dizzy. With shaking hands, she puts down the camera and takes off her clothes. Then she finds a condom and wraps up his cock.

He's breathing fast behind the mask. Slowly, bracing herself on his hard thighs, she lowers herself onto his shaft. His cock feels almost too big at first as her pussy stretches around him. Already something wet and portentous is building inside her, like a water balloon about to break. Then they start thrusting together and she stares at the mask and Adam's eyes stare back and for a few hallucinogenic moments, she feels like she's teleported into her own *King Slut* porn movie. She's fucking the god of her pornographic dreams, at last. Various scenes she's directed flash through her mind as she plays with her clit and then her orgasm breaks between her legs, hot and wet. Adam follows with a long groan.

Her limbs feel like jelly but she lifts off the mask and uncuffs him before collapsing on the sheets. Adam falls next to her, a mess of damp black hair and flushed skin. "I thought you wanted the mask on."

"Right now I want you."

The room is hot, almost stifling, but he holds her close. Both of them are wet and trembling and a little weak. As he begins touching her, a new current forms in the dark between them, running from her fingertips to Adam's skin and back again. It's the new voltage of her pornographic sphere, a nexus of flesh and bone and her own real porn god beside her.

PICTURE ME NAKED

Velvet Moore

I slide my leg across a worn patch and circle a finger around a cigarette burn etched into the faded magenta leather, toying a bit with the piece of foam poking out. It's now that I wish I had a picture of myself. I'd fold it neatly and slip it between the seat cushions with enough of a corner peeking through to get noticed. I'd hope the next stop after me would be at a hotel where a businessman in a wrinkled gray suit would be catching a ride to the airport for a red-eye flight back to parenting and paperwork. He'd find the picture and toy with it like the seat foam, running fingertips along the image. He'd store it in his carry-on bag and pray he wouldn't be asked to pull it out at the security screening. He would be embarrassed to have to publicly reveal a photo of my slick, spreading thighs and have to explain it to authorities. I'd pray that he does.

These thoughts excite me from my brain stem to my bottom, and I consider moving the toying fingers from the seat to work their way down my pants and rub one out right here in the back of this cab. Weeks ago, I wouldn't have been so brave.

Weeks ago, I picked up a bag of items I had left at my ex's after moving out. Having been a jerk, he had left my stuff on his front porch in a plastic grocery bag with my name scribbled in with permanent marker. I shifted through its contents at the coffee shop a few blocks from his house: my phone charger, cracked turquoise earrings, clothes and a coffee cup with the corner of something poking out of the rim. I tugged the corner and it popped out like a rattlesnake snapping from behind a rock. And there I was, nude, sprawled on his bed, pink nipple in hand, begging him forward. A moment captured in privacy, unexpectedly revealed in public.

I wore my irritation for him like a weight belt the rest of the day. Why did he leave my stuff on the porch in a bag that could have easily passed as garbage? Anyone could have grabbed that bag. I slowly rotated my head, letting the hot beads of water from the showerhead roll down my shoulders. The thoughts consumed me as I soaped. Not even the liquid heat was helping to reduce my tension. What if someone had picked that up off of his porch? Why didn't he warn me so I wouldn't open it in a public place? What if someone had seen it over my shoulder? Would it have been a happy surprise with their grande latte? Would they think my milky cream skin was a lovely complement to coffee?

My soapy hands rounded along my full breasts making quick swipes then slowing, molding me like his had done when he put the camera down. I slid one hand down and squeezed my inner thigh and dragged two fingers along my lips as my other hand worked its way back to my chest. He always had the most talented hands. I looked down, seeing my nipples perky despite the shower's heat. I rolled them each between my fingers. This is what he saw. My nipples like life rafts floating in a sea of flesh, surrounded and begging to be tugged. This is what the trash man would have seen. This is what the coffee drinker would have seen. I twisted my tight little nipples until the pressure tingled its way down to my center.

After my shower, I found myself one part irritated, two parts intrigued. I couldn't clear my mind of the thought that someone could have seen that photo of me, and what that person might have felt after finding it. The more I thought about it, the more I liked the fact that I might have interjected the idea of sex into his or her day. I slipped out of bed and grabbed my digital camera from my purse. Climbing back under the covers, I clicked on the camera and switched off the light. I shimmied out of my panties and threw off my gown. Then I lifted the sheet and snapped a shot of the length of my nude body, stretched out and bright white from the flash.

In the morning, I printed the picture from my home computer, folded it twice and traveled with it back to the coffee shop near my ex's house. The barista handed me a tall hot chocolate and a muffin and when he wasn't looking, I dropped the picture into his tip jar.

That night, the camera got a little closer, with my knees bent, tenting the bedsheet and the lens pointing directly between my thighs. That one I posted on the coffee shop bulletin board, hidden partially behind a flier offering dog-walking services. A shot of me on my hands and knees would have been more suitable, I mused.

Imagination is the ability to form mental images, sensations and concepts in a moment when your senses fail you for information. You can close your eyes and imagine how a woman might appear embarrassed to find a photo of your naked breasts when she opens her dinner menu. Can you see the confusion creep across her face, then the blush trickle to her chest, flushing bright against the plunging neckline of her black dress? Then see her forehead crease as disgust sets in. Picture the way her husband pretends to agree with her dismay as she shoves it his way, him trying not to look too closely at this seemingly disgusting image. See him pressing his wide palm against his awakened crotch as his wife yells for the waiter's assistance.

I thought of that palm all night as I sprawled naked between the cool, thin cotton sheets, pressing my fingers against slick folds as I imagine he might have desired. I can't be sure who got the menu I laced that night; yet, whether or not they planned to order accordingly, it seems they got the special.

Menus are easy to access, I discovered. Whether it's a coffee shop or a fancy restaurant, there is plenty opportunity to insert yourself into people's lives. That's why they became the scene of my first few experiments. You see, what my ex had unwittingly taught me by leaving that photo in public is that there is a fine line between embarrassment and eroticism. The body language of surprise is similar to the body language of sex: widened eyes, gasping, trembling, mouth dropping open, the sharp jolt of tension that passes through your chest. If approached correctly, what may have originally surprised then embarrassed you can be redirected to surprise and excite you.

The last of the restaurant rotation I left inside the seat of the piano bench at a seafood place that featured live music on Saturday nights. On top of the sheet music was a distant shot of my ass, glowing with handprints. The camera's timer had come in handy and with every second countdown, I slapped my skin a little harder, priming myself for the perfect shot. Maybe the piano man would find it after a long night of playing, hide it from his bandmates and stop in the restroom before his drive home. Leaning against the chilly marble countertop, he would sweep his hand along his cock like playing a slide trombone, picturing his pelvis bumping against my strawberry cheeks and making my sweet cunt sing.

I toured an open house in a nearby neighborhood, posing as an interested homebuyer. Inside one of the kitchen drawers I left a new photo of me. The realtor revealed that the house was move-in ready since the previous owners had already moved into their new home. So move in I did...on a dark-haired couple who was also touring. "This may sound strange," I said to them when they stopped to examine the kitchen sink fixtures. "But you two look great in this house. Something about it just suits you." Later I pictured them as happy new homeowners, him wearing a paint-stained alma mater T-shirt and her in short shorts, surrounded by boxes and trying to settle into this new house. She would be putting away knives and spoons and discover a folded picture of legs in fishnets straddling a kitchen chair. "Honey, come and see this," she would say. He would enter, stand behind her and wrap one arm around her small waist, using the other to hold out the photo for examination. "Hmm," he would mutter as they stood in contemplation for a moment longer, until she started slowly grinding her rear into him and he pulled firmly against her waist, pressing himself harder into her. Quickly her short shorts would be down and his T-shirt would be flung and they would fuck on the kitchen counter, her hands reaching above her head to grab the shiny sink fixtures for leverage.

Sitting naked on my bedroom floor, I lathered my feet up to my calves in baby oil, leaving them slick and shining. Then I sat cross-legged, being careful not to block too much of my naked center from the camera lens. I carefully threaded a pearl necklace between my toes, beads becoming slick as they passed through. I shaped the trailing end of the necklace into a heart. *Click*.

I walked onto the first floor of a nearby hotel and dropped the photo, sealed in a manila envelope, at the doorstep of room

169. It seems the lucky resident got a side order of my glossy toes and plump clit with his room service. In the hotel locker room adjacent to the pool I slipped the string of pearls between my legs and rubbed along folds slicker than baby oil.

Then I needed to see my viewers: once, with the photo taped to the front of a TV on display as I watched for reactions from the next aisle over; once with it shoved under the windshield wipers of a four-door sedan with me watching from my rearview mirror; once, gripping my breast in hand while my newspaper blocked my unbuttoned blouse. I had to see who would be so lucky as to pick up the newspaper in which I had hidden my photo.

Tonight there is no newspaper kiosk. No locker room. No open house. Tonight I can only wish for a businessman in a wrinkled gray suit and the picture he might hide away. I'm meeting my brother downtown for dinner and I intend to play it straight. No camera. No pictures. No photo of my ass in a thong slipped at someone's feet under a bathroom stall door. No shot of an ice cube clutched and melting between my knees. No hiding it under a neighboring plate.

The cab slows as it approaches the restaurant and I slide forward on the magenta leather seat, leaning in to see the tally I owe. The tires stop and I'm pulling out money, but the driver clears the meter to zero. I'm confused. "What do I owe you," I'm asking, while catching his eyes in the rearview mirror. "Not money," he says, and his hand is traveling from the meter to his upper thigh, gripping muscle and jeans as one big handful.

I'm still confused as I look again at the meter then at something poking out of the dashboard. And now I see it. The picture I thought was still with my phone charger and cracked turquoise earrings. The picture I had opened by surprise in a coffee cup from an ex-lover. The picture of me tweaking perky, pink nipples.

The picture that must have slipped from a plastic grocery bag during my ride home weeks ago. The picture I didn't intentionally leave behind. The sun-faded picture now stuck in a crack in the dirty dashboard of this cab. This stranger, who has me behind locked doors, is picturing me naked. On his dashboard and in his backseat, I am wide-eyed and breathless.

WANT

Alison Tyler

"Just leave my stuff alone."

"I didn't touch your stupid stuff."

"Liar."

"Bitch."

We used to be friends, Lia and me. We were tight. We could hang out all day long and still have things to talk about in the evening over a beer, or a margarita, or a cosmopolitan. But when we moved in together, everything changed. Her personality—always larger than life—seemed to spill into every corner of the apartment. I felt as if I couldn't exist in any room except my own. And even there, she'd track me down, stomping into my private haven, spreading her Opium scent everywhere.

"Did you move my hair dryer?"

"Of course not." I have short hair. I let my curls dry naturally. I'd have no need to touch her styling tools.

"Did you take my shoes?"

"Why would I take your shoes? We don't even wear the same

style." Lia was all about sky-high heels, while I favored battered motorcycle boots.

She was always accusatory, and finally, I simply stopped talking to her.

Our other roommate, Vincent, didn't like the behavior. "You're not going to speak?"

I shrugged.

"To me, too?"

"Well, you're fucking her, so you're going to take her side, aren't you?"

That was actually my biggest problem. Lia had moved in with the two of us. And in a week, she and Vince had started up a relationship. They fucked on the kitchen table, on the sofa, in the shower. I hadn't wanted to look too hard at what was annoying me the most—because I think if I had, I'd have seen such a strong streak of jealousy in me that I wouldn't have been able to drown the emerald monster in my beer.

Vincent's eyes took on a strange glow, and he simply patted me on the head as if I were a stray dog and walked out of the kitchen. I sighed and grabbed another Heineken. So it was only three p.m. It was five o'clock somewhere.

That night, Vince came into my room. I was wearing my headset so I wouldn't have to listen to the two of them howl, and I was typing on my computer. I didn't look up. I didn't even acknowledge his presence until he ran his thumb over my iPod and shut down my volume. The move was strangely erotic. I could imagine his thumb running just that softly over my clit.

"What's up?"

That same look was in his eyes. Christ, he was so goddamn handsome. Why did he have to look like that? Why did he have to be so doable and go for her instead of me?

"I want to apologize."

Now, I settled back in my chair. I was intrigued. "For what?"

"For Lia's behavior."

"Shouldn't she be the one to apologize?"

"She will. I assure you. But I have to say, I didn't stop her from treating you badly. She's been rude and inconsiderate and, you know, bitchy. But she's going to pay for that."

"What do you mean?"

"Well, tonight, you're going to listen to me punishing her."

Had I been mildly interested before? If I had suddenly turned into a cartoon, my eyes would have bugged out of my head and my tongue would have lolled between my lips. In reality, I simply leaned forward, as if quietly intrigued.

Our bedrooms were connected to a bathroom. Vincent went to the wall and opened the adjoining door. Then he walked through the small tiled space and cracked the door that led to his room.

"You can stand in the bathroom. Sit on the counter. Press your face to the slit. Whatever you want. You'll be able to eavesdrop on Lia's discipline."

I was instantly wet. I couldn't tell if Vincent knew, but I felt the dampness in my panties. I crossed my legs, and Vincent smiled.

"Of course, there'll be a payment involved."

"What do you mean?" Did he expect me to give him money?

"Tomorrow night, she'll get to hear you."

"Get to hear me what?"

"Get to hear you cry."

My thoughts felt molasses slow, dark and thick. "What are you talking about?"

His lips curled into a smile. He seemed to appreciate my feistiness. In a very patient tone he said, "Tomorrow night, Lia will get to listen to me punishing you. I'm going to put you over my lap and turn your pale cheeks the color of a red, velvety rose."

How had he guessed that at night I fantasized about a man spanking me? That the thought of handcuffs turned me on? That the image of a dominant man in control was all I ever needed to get off…? Vincent's eyes were such a pretty green. I stared at him and imagined him doing all those things to me. But then I remembered what he'd proposed. The thought of her getting pleasure from my pain made me shake my head.

"No way."

Vincent laughed, which incensed me.

"No fucking way," I repeated, adding the expletive to let him know my feelings. I was so pissed at her. We'd been friends. There was no way on earth I was going to let her enjoy the sound of her boyfriend spanking me. What did he think I was? A tool?

"You're going to change your mind," he said.

"What makes you think I'd let you do that to me?"

"Same reason she's going to let me do it to her. You want it." And then he left the room.

Well, fuck him. I slammed the door to the bathroom. Let them have their own kinky little spank fest. I would have no part of it. I put my headset back on and returned to my typing. I'd been hired to abridge an ancient Chinese morality fable, and I knew that I could easily lose myself in my work. At least, I could until the sound of Lia crying out reached me even through the earphones. First, I turned up the volume. Come on, Anthony. You and your Peppers have more power than a bitchy blonde, don't you? I got closer to the computer. I continued nipping and tucking—a word here, a line there. I had to cut nearly a third of the book—but my first pass was in slow, steady spanks. I mean, slices. Fucking hell.

Her cries increased in volume. I responded by turning my sound up louder. I could feel the rhythm in my core.

But then the song ended. And before the next one started up, I could hear her. I let my thumb caress the volume control. I thought of Vincent's big hands. I turned off the iPod.

Would they know if I moved into the bathroom, if I got closer so I could really hear and maybe see? They couldn't possibly. I stood and walked as quietly as I'd ever walked before across the floor. The sounds in the other room didn't stop, didn't pause, didn't change in any way. Silently, I opened the door to the bathroom and stepped inside. The noises were louder now—sobs and sighs. I stood entirely still. Had they heard me? Did they know I had given up all sense of decorum and headed into no-man's-land?

If anything, the sound of Lia's cries upped in intensity. There was no way either one of them could have heard my stockinged footsteps.

Still, I held my breath as I tiptoed my way across the cold tiled floor then aligned my face with the crack in the door and peered inside. There were candles. Everywhere. Who knew Vincent was so romantic? That fact made me hate Lia even more. Fat ivory candles burned on the windowsill. Twisted black spirals flickered on the dresser. Candlelight provided the only illumination in the room—but it was enough. Enough for me to see...

My thighs clenched involuntarily. I felt a jolt of arousal zing through me. I'd never watched anyone fuck before. Never eavesdropped. Never peeked. No, they weren't fucking—not yet, anyway. But what they were doing was definitely a turn-on.

Vincent had Lia over his lap, and he was punishing her sweet, sassy ass with a paddle. I'd seen that ass swish down the hallway. I had seen it when she'd bent over to unload the laundry, seen it when she went prancing out the door in a far-too-short, schoolgirl skirt, which I now saw was in a crumpled ball on the floor. But this was my favorite time. Because he was wielding that paddle with finesse, and Lia continued to cry out and kick her heels and pound her fists uselessly in protest. Or mock protest. I wondered if she could have gotten free if she had tried hard enough. But then I saw Vincent grimace and grab both of her hands in one of his. He pinned her wrists neatly at the small of her back and then let go a volley of blows on her hindquarters.

Damn. That must have hurt.

I swallowed hard, and then I did something completely unexpected—to me, anyway. I put one hand down under the waistband of my yoga pants, and I touched my clit. Just touched it, mind you. I didn't rub. I didn't press. I simply set my middle finger right against my clit and watched.

Vincent discarded the paddle on the bed and lifted Lia in his arms. Was he going to console her? Was he going to kiss away her tears? No. He moved her so that she was right in the center of their bed, and he picked up a pair of handcuffs.

Holy hell. This was getting better by the second; at least for me, if not Lia. Because she looked a bit scared as Vincent moved on to bind her ankles to the footboard. I was starting to really enjoy myself. But then a thought occurred to me. He had told me that tonight I could listen to Lia, and tomorrow night... I pushed that thought out of my head. There was no way he could make me. No way they could force me...not if I didn't want them to.

And yet, I was starting to change my mind about that, because as I watched, Vincent stripped out of his clothes. Oh, he was so handsome—too handsome. I stared as he opened up a bottle of lube and poured a puddle into his palm. Lia began to strain against the bindings. I guess she'd thought he was simply going to fuck her. Vincent clearly had his own ideas.

"If you fight, things will go worse for you," he said.

The finger, which had only been resting on my clit, began to make slow circles, as if with a mind of its own. I wasn't telling myself to make those circles. I was doing no instructing at all.

I watched, mesmerized, as Vincent jacked his hand up and down his cock, getting the head and shaft all wet with the lube. Then he spread Lia's asscheeks and ran his fingertips between them.

"No…" she murmured.

"Yes…" he responded.

I watched, swallowing hard, as Vincent got behind her on the bed and used both hands now to spread her asscheeks wide apart—as he pushed the head of his cock into what I could only guess was her tight little asshole.

Lia cried out. Vincent made soothing noises to her under his breath. I imagined him fucking me like that, envisioned him putting me over his lap and spanking my ass and then preparing me just as he was preparing her, and then… Oh, god, I was going to come. I was. Right there in the bathroom, no better than any other peeping Tom. I shut my eyes. I listened to her whimper, and I let myself go.

Quietly, as quietly as I possibly could, I slipped back to my room.

I was still telling myself that they didn't have to know what I'd done, that there was no way they could force me to reciprocate.

But I didn't believe me. I've never been a good liar.

In the morning, I didn't leave my bed. I waited for both of my roommates to get dressed, make coffee and head off to their respective offices. Then I tiptoed my way down the hall to snag a cup of joe for myself. I was surprised by what I saw on the kitchen table.

A schoolgirl skirt.

Lia's schoolgirl skirt.

Pinned to the hem was a note:

If you want to play, you have to dress the part.

What did that mean? Well, I knew what it meant. Put on the skirt if I wanted to have what happened to Lia happen to me. And I did. Sort of. I wanted Vincent to do all those naughty, nasty things to me. But I didn't want Lia to have the pleasure of watching. So I was torn. And what if the skirt didn't fit me?

I held up the red-and-black plaid. The hem reached only the tops of my thighs. This was barely long enough to be called a mini.

It wouldn't hurt to try on the skirt. That wasn't agreeing to anything. Nobody was home. I stripped off my yoga pants and slid on the skirt, buttoned the side. The skirt seemed even shorter once I had it on. But it fit.

I was about to take the thing off again, when I had second thoughts. Nobody would know if I wore the skirt for a little while. Nobody would know if I went into my bedroom, grabbed my vibrator and made myself come while I had the skirt on. Who would tell Vincent? The skirt? My dildo?

If I couldn't participate in their little ménage à fuck, I could at least get off at the thought. I went to the bedroom and snagged my toy from the bedside table. With images from the previous night still fresh in my mind, I sprawled on the bed and started to touch myself. I worked slowly, not turning on the vibrator at first, just running the toy up and down between my legs, over my panties, pressing hard on my clit.

Finally, I turned on the motor and slid aside my panties. Oh, god, that felt good. The fabric of the skirt was a little scratchy against my bare thighs, and for some reason, I liked that. There was sex in this skirt. I thought of Lia wearing the naughty outfit.

I thought of the way she'd looked when Vincent had punished her. I imagined being the one over his lap, feeling his hand drag up the hem, feeling his palm on my ass. I...

"Thought so."

Jesus Christ.

Vincent was standing in the doorway of my bedroom. At first, I tried to feign indignation. But indignation—or anything else, for that matter—is a difficult emotion to slip into when you are spread-eagled on your bed with a toy in your twat.

"Don't stop on my account."

I stared at him and swallowed hard. I didn't think I could make myself come while he was watching. And yet I didn't think I could stop myself from coming regardless of who was watching. Even if that who turned out to be Lia, who stepped into the doorway next to him.

Damn.

"Keep going," Lia said softly. "You look so pretty."

What were they doing back? They were supposed to be at work! Lia took a step into the room, and I just stared. Was she going to say something snide, like always? Was she going to tell me that I wasn't handling the vibrator correctly?

No, she sat on the edge of the bed and started to stroke my legs. I stared at her. Sure, she was beautiful. I'd always thought so. But the last few months had made her ugly in my mind. Such a know-it-all. And so bossy. Yet she wasn't being bossy now, she was being helpful, her fingers running up and down my inner thighs.

"Why don't you let Lia work the vibrator?"

That was Vincent. He was being helpful, too.

"I don't think you should let her come yet," Lia said, as if I'd agreed to something. As if we were all on the same page. "I think you should spank her first. She is wearing my skirt after all."

My fingers clenched hard on the dildo. If the motorized toy had been human, it would have squealed in protest. Vincent smiled at me. "I think that's a good idea," he said and came toward the bed. Now was the time for me to flee. Now was the time for me to say, "Hell, no, you freaks. I don't know what kind of a girl you think I am, but I'm not the kind who would willingly bend over her roommate's lap and..."

Vincent had sat down in my desk chair. He was looking at me expectantly. Lia gently pried my fingers from around the vibrator and turned off the toy. They were both waiting for me. Meekly, I stood up and adjusted my panties, smoothed the wrinkles in the pleated skirt. I could still run. They wouldn't expect that. I could turn on my heel and sprint down the hall to safety.

Vincent patted his lap. I walked to his side and lay down over his knees. He palmed my ass through the schoolgirl skirt and then gave me one practice spank. The fabric of my knickers and the plaid skirt muffled the sensation. He lifted the hem and then spanked me through my underwear. I continued to spin myself an imaginary story in which I told my roommates I wasn't interested in playing naughty games with them, that I was perfectly happy in my loner lifestyle.

His hand came down harder, and I squealed. Damn, that hurt, but not as bad as the one that followed. When he started to pull my panties down, I squirmed on his lap.

"Don't fight me," he said, and his tone had gone menacing. "Things will go much harder for you if you do."

Then my panties were down, and he was spanking me. For real. This is what a spanking felt like: pain and pain and more pain and the most undeniable sultry pleasure of all time. I had no idea anything could feel like this. The spanks stung, but my pussy responded in the craziest way. I could feel the pulse between my legs. Vincent seemed to understand, because after delivering a volley of blows, he let his fingertips probe between my pussy lips, and he came up with a wealth of wetness.

"Look at that, Lia," he said, "she's all drippy."

Lia strode forward. "Can I taste?"

I assumed she was licking my juices off his fingers. But then he spread my thighs wide apart, and I felt her tongue directly on me. On my clit. I was undone. Lia's sweet tongue made darting circles around my clit. Her face was thrust between my legs. I could not catch my breath. The sensation was overwhelming. My hot ass. Her darling tongue. Vincent's hands stroking my hair. But before I could come, Vincent said, "Let's move to the bed."

He lifted me up and carried me—not to my bed but to his. Before I could say a word, he had me bound, as he'd had her bound. I was still wearing a T-shirt and that magic skirt. But before he tied my ankles, he pulled my panties all the way off.

"Do you want to let her come once?" he asked Lia. "Before I fuck her ass?"

No, no, no, no, no! my mind screamed. *Yes, yes, yes, yes, yes,* replied my body.

"Please," Lia murmured. Then she was back between my thighs, suckling and nipping and licking until I could take no more.

"I'm going to…" I started.

"Of course, you are," said Vincent. Lia didn't move her mouth from me until the contractions subsided. And then Vincent took her place. I felt the lube. I felt his cock. I closed my eyes.

"Look at me," Lia said. She was sitting in front of me now, stroking my curls from my forehead. "Stare at me while he fucks you."

"It's going to hurt."

"It always does," she agreed. "But then…"

And Vincent pressed forward. I could feel his cock stretching me open. I could feel the pain sear through me. Almost immediately, the pleasure followed, at being filled, at being taken, at having been punished.

"You like it," Lia breathed. "Oh, god, girl. You like it."

I did. There was no denying. Vincent pounded into me, and I cried out. Lia moved to the side of our bodies, and she slid a hand under me, so that each time I ground my hips forward, I was grinding against her knuckles. When Vincent came, emptying himself into me, I came, too. Hard. On Lia's hand.

Then I collapsed, tied to his bed, demolished by my two roommates. Lia undid the bindings. Vincent undressed me and wrapped me up in one of his sheets. We all lay there on the bed, stunned and pleased—but far from finished.

"You ought to punish Lia next," I said to Vincent as he threw his arm around me.

"Why?"

I gazed at my roommate. "She's wearing my shoes."

TRICKS

Lola Olson

The dress was far too short for me. I knew that well. The hem
rode up my thigh every four or five steps I took. I tried to walk
slowly, balancing dangerously on the tall heels on my feet. It was
obvious to anyone looking that I had no idea what on earth I
was doing in them and how I managed to make more than five
steps easily was anybody's guess.

I bundled myself as best I could in the small jacket that barely
covered my chest. The red dress was as busty as it was short,
and a small blush surfaced on my cheeks when I realized anyone
watching could see glimpses of my cleavage as easily as they could
my fishnet stockings. Keeping my pace steady, I walked through
the brisk air toward the street corner where I knew he would
be. Short brown hair and blue eyes, my friend had told me. She
wouldn't tell how she found him or where she met him, but when
I told her what I was looking for, she assured me he was it.

When I reached the right block, my stomach sank. He wasn't
there. The spot was empty. All of this preparation, my overdra-
matic makeup, these wretched heels, the risk I ran to walk up

and down the street looking like this...everything I had done for nothing. Tilting on my heel and nearly falling over for the fifteenth time, I spotted a figure in an alleyway highlighted by a small red cigarette spark.

My heartbeat raced when I saw a flicker of red light fall to the ground. Summoning the best of my courage, I opened my jacket and walked toward the spark as sexily as I could muster. Smelling his cologne as I stepped closer, I heard my voice tremble when I said, "Hello, Officer."

His cigarette fell to the street and he stepped forward in the light. He was exactly as she described him, but better. He tilted his black hat at me, revealing some of his brown hair. His eyes twinkled at me as he smiled. "Can I help you, Madame?"

I wondered if he could see my face turn red as goose bumps peppered my cleavage. I couldn't decide if I wanted him to or not. Grabbing at courage from somewhere I couldn't fathom, I stuck my chest out farther and winked at him. "I was wondering if I could help you actually, Officer." Hearing the words coming out of my mouth heated my cheeks. They felt as ridiculous as they sounded.

"I'm not sure what you're implying, Madame."

"What I mean to say is," I began, dropping my short jacket on the ground, "I would be glad to help you." I slid my hands over his vest, pushing my knee in between his legs, "for the right price of course."

He pulled away quickly, looking at me with widened eyes, a reaction I expected. I could tell by the folded lines on his brow that whatever he was feeling was a mixture of disgust, shock and something I could and would definitely enjoy putting my finger on.

"Madame, you're operating under some huge misconceptions," he said.

"Am I?" I asked.

"Yes," he said firmly.

"That's not what I heard," I said, overcoming my fear slowly but surely. The more I was playing the part, the more I felt it.

"Is that a fact?"

"It is. I heard you got around with lots of us. I heard you were known for that, actually," I said.

He grabbed me suddenly, pulling me away from where the alley opened into the street and back into the dark, shoving me against the wall, bricks scraping my skin slightly. He held me by my forearms against the wall, anger coloring his cheeks.

"You heard wrong," he said, an edge coating his voice.

"Did I?" I said, trying to seem unfazed by the sudden force of the exchange. The waver of my voice and the heat building beneath my skirt hinted that I was very, very fazed.

"Yes," he said, tightening his grip. "I'm an upstanding man of the law."

A thought scurried through my mind and made me smile and I knew the perfect thing to say.

"What are you laughing at?" he said threateningly.

"Well," I began, giving him my best smile, "I heard you were upstanding but...in quite the different way." I started to laugh a little when his eyebrows furrowed. He yanked me from the wall, pulled my wrists to my lower back and pushed me down the alleyway. The cool air rushed past my legs as I walked through the darkness until I felt a roughness on my thighs near my knees that felt like corduroy fabric. He shoved me down face-first into a cushy pillow covered by it. I realized as I heard the clank of metal that he had me bent over the arm of some two-seated sofa...a bad smelling two-seated sofa.

"You're going to pay for that," he said, wrapping the cold steel around my wrists, binding my arms back. The seconds seemed like minutes when he released me, and I couldn't feel the warmth of his rough pants on the back of my legs. If I could have balled my wrists into the rough fabric my face was scratching against, I would have. The anticipation pooled in my stomach and seeped toward my groin. Even though my legs were tightly shut and straight so I could maintain what little balance I had, I knew I was getting wet.

I felt a knee shoved roughly between my legs. "Spread," he said softly but harshly. I felt the air hit my thighs when he shoved up my red dress, then nothing again for a while, not even any clinking metal sounds. My heartbeat drummed in my ears slowly as I waited. I wanted to beg, but I didn't know what I should be begging for.

I inhaled sharply when the first blow hit where my thighs met my ass and then again when another blow striped across it in the center, nearing the bone and sending a wave of pain that splayed white across the backs of my eyelids.

"Got any other clever words?" he asked from behind me, swinging the baton and inching farther toward the bone. "Any more clever quips for me, whore?"

The metal of the baton felt cool against my thighs for brief periods between the snapping and clicking strokes. Even if I had wanted to speak, my breath was gone. He landed several more blows before he paused. "Have you had enough, slut?" I caught my breath again and cracked a smile. When the pain dulled its constant throbbing, I felt a throbbing of a different kind. A small breeze brushed across my ass, reminding me of how hot his baton had made me. My red dress must've looked so wrinkled and my thong displaced.

"I haven't actually," I said, reveling in the long inhales I had taken. "I think I want more."

Just as I finished speaking, I felt the baton snap again against my ass. The throbbing pain began to match the pulses of blood that had to be pumping through my labia and clit. I could feel them growing warm under the assault. The beating stopped when a low moan ghosted out of my mouth, and I would have given anything to see his expression. He paused before he roughly shoved the loose material of my panties aside, digging his fingers into me, spreading my wetness around. I heard him inhale sharply. "You're enjoying this, aren't you?" he said angrily. "You're getting off on it like some twisted, dirty whore."

His fingers felt electric under my labia, swirling around and seeming anything but disgusted. He paused, resting on my clit before pushing against it, firmly and quickly, making me moan again at the sudden speed. "Yes," I said, both at his statement and at the motions of his hand, moaning again when he pulled away. He traced his hands farther up my thigh, yanking down the tacky tights I had picked out the week before. They had been wrapped in cheap plastic, hanging on a rack in the store. When I bought them I felt a tingling mix of embarrassment and anticipation as I stood at the cash register in my business casual clothes. What would everyone in my office think if they saw me in these tacky fishnet tights? I stuck my ass out at the feeling as he shoved the tights down to my ankles, pulling them off my feet.

"If you're going to act like a whore, I'm going to treat you like one," he said roughly, before shoving my thighs apart. I tried to find footing on the ground as I heard him unzip his pants. My arms were growing sore and the pattern of the rough corduroy felt etched into my face. I wasn't prepared to feel his cock against my ass so quickly, while my thong was still barely on. It felt as warm as my ass did. "Do you like this?" he asked me, reaching up, twisting my thong in his hands, "Or do you want more?"

I didn't even wait for a pause. "More, please," I said quickly, while he pulled my thong slowly down. "What was that?" he said. My underwear fell to the ground as he pulled my hips farther away from the couch my face went down, buried in the fabric. It smelled even riper than before, but it was the last sense I was focusing on. He pushed his cock underneath me, so it was sliding up and down my labia. "Say it," he said, "Louder."

"I want it," I said loud and clear, "Please...Officer." He dragged his cock up and down, brushing my clit softly. "You do want it," he said, "don't you? You hungry little cock-whore. You want me to fuck you in this filthy alley, shove my cock in your pussy?"

"Yes," I said, feeling a nervous sheen of sweat form between my breasts. "Yes, Sir. Please fuck me."

He slid his cock into me quickly, wet from where it had been brushing up against me. Just as when he beat me, he didn't give me time to think before he started pumping his hips. When he pushed in roughly, I could feel the pleasure pooling, moving from where his cock was and leaking into my clit. It burned, begging to be touched. Even his fingertips gripping my hips felt good. "You like this, don't you?" he whispered in my ear. "Filthy slut." His words made my nerves crack and tingle, sending the pleasure flowing from my pussy in waves as thick and sweet as sugary syrup, and I could do nothing but let it escape my mouth in small groans. Even if I could have moved my hands, I wouldn't have wanted to.

I could hear another sharp inhalation in my ear as he leaned forward and grabbed my shoulders, pushing harder, making the pleasure burn quickly. I could feel it welling up and building, like rough waters behind a strong dam. "Please don't stop, Sir," I begged, not even realizing what I was saying.

"Take it then," he responded, leaning against me again. "Take it, you fucking whore."

I could feel an orgasm welling deeper again as the words thrummed in my ears, but a small sound pulled me back from it. He slowed his thrusts and the waves retreated. I couldn't believe my ears. His cell phone was ringing. Of all things, his bloody cell phone. I wanted to scream and curse, and I nearly began to before he popped it open.

"Hello?" he said, still pulling in and out slowly and chuckling softly. "What am I doing? Fucking a filthy whore in a dingy alleyway." I knew I should have been angry, but something other than anger was pulsing through my veins.

"Why don't you come by?" he said. "You can have a go with her." I felt my face color again.

Blood thumped through my ears as he continued his conversation, still slowly pushing in and out of me. Part of me thought this was near blasphemy, that I should push myself off that dingy couch, demand to be taken out of the handcuffs, gather my panties and what was left of my dignity and storm off. Part of me liked what little friction I had and thought it was worth staying around for more, despite the rudeness. And then there was another part of me that liked what he was doing, his blasé disregard for my feelings, the fact that the rumors were true and the fact that I was special enough to share.

"No, this one's on the house, I won't charge you," he said, pausing before continuing. "She's a petite brunette in the tartiest outfit you've ever seen, and I'd bet you a fiver she's got the tightest pussy you've ever fucked."

I tightened myself instinctively, all of the warm and sweet feelings pooling into my clit again. I kept quiet, hoping the conversation would continue and inspire him to check me for any features the caller wanted in particular. I got extraordinarily lucky.

"You'd think she would be, but she's not. And she's easy too."

His hands moved past my thighs directly to my labia, rubbing a few amazing circles around my clit. "She got wet at nearly the drop of a hat and she should still be. You could probably go for hours on her, and she begs beautifully, too." He laughed in agreement with his friend, pulling away and stopping all of his movements. I moaned in slight protest, and he pushed his hand onto the small of my back. "Don't interrupt me," he whispered.

It was anguishing, the last few minutes of his phone call, even more because they didn't invite more of his touch on me. He kept his hand on the small of my back the whole time, letting me inhale more ripe fumes from the sofa without even his cock in me to sate me a little. He had pulled it out when I had foolishly interrupted. I cursed under my breath.

"I'll see you in five, yeah? I'll keep her warm for you," he said, clicking the phone closed, finally.

He moved his hand from the small of my back and placed both on my wrists, digging the metal into my skin just slightly as he leaned toward my ear. "I should just let you sit here and stew for that. You interrupted a very important phone call. I don't just waltz about the streets all day, you know. I have business to attend to. I gave you the privilege of fucking you while I talked, and you had the audacity to try and interrupt. What have you to say for yourself?"

"I'm sorry," I said, without missing a beat. I didn't feel like being coy or playing any more games. I just wanted something, whatever he had to give me, "I'm sorry I interrupted...Officer. It won't happen again."

I could hear the smile in his voice. "You are very well trained, aren't you? Let's see if we can soften you up a little before the others arrive." I wanted to ask who the others were, but when he pushed his cock into me again, I honestly didn't care about anything but the oddly satisfying feeling of fullness when he shoved himself forward. It tickled but made me feel like I was melting from the inside out. And when he pulled me back just so to slide his warm fingers over my clit, up and down, pushing just slightly, it turned the tickle into a fire that made my pulse quicken. I could feel my body picking up where it had left off, drawing up so quickly I was sad to think it was coming to an end.

Instantly, I could feel my pussy tighten and send sparks shooting through my clit and labia and on up through my chest in a wave. Taking a breath in instinctively, I held on to it so it would last longer, exhaling only slightly to continue to ride the feeling of waves and circuits shorting through my system. I could never understand how women in movies could scream so loud when they came. In the short twenty-five years of my life, no matter how much I moaned and took breaths between my teeth while being fucked or fucking, coming had always felt so strong it stole my breath away.

Out of the corner of my eye, I could pick up flashing blue and red lights as I caught my breath. Before I could sort it out, something black had been draped over my eyelids. "Very good," he whispered in my ear. "You've softened up nice, haven't you? Now stay here and keep quiet for me while I go talk with them, hmm? Be a good little slut for me."

I nodded quickly and mumbled, "Yes, Officer," as best I could.

He zipped his pants up and walked a few steps away. I could still hear his voice over the thumping in my ears.

"Where's your partner?"

"I'm not sure I could bring him just yet, and the other guys wanted me to vouch for you. You know how the last girl you had went."

He groaned. "That was weeks ago. And I told you, this one is different."

Their voices paused as their footsteps drew closer. There she is," he said, "As good as I described her, even better."

"She looks a bit disheveled," the voice said. "What did you do to her?"

"Just softened her up a little bit for you so you won't have to waste any time."

"Look at those heels. She was quite tarted up, wasn't she?"

"She's even more tarted up now," he said, moving my hips over slightly. I heard the other man take a sharp breath through his teeth. He brushed his hands roughly between my asscheeks and down my labia, pushing past them to explore as they burned to his touch. I wanted to move my hips to guide his fingers to my clit, but I kept as still as I could.

"Damn," he said, stepping a bit closer. "She's nice and slick, isn't she?"

"As I promised," the first cop said.

He dipped his fingers into my pussy, pushing them in and out slowly but steadily. "She's still nice and tight, too, even after you've had a go?"

"I told you, didn't I? I don't call you unless it's for the good girls. This one's good. She begs really nice too. Push her clit a few times, and she'll say any fucking thing you want."

The new arrival leaned his weight on my back a little, pulling his fingers out of me and gripping my hip with his hand. As he lined his hips against mine, he ground himself into me a little, letting me feel that he was hard. He shoved his other hand in front of me, pushing his fingers past my labia, finding my clit easily, and rubbing hard and fast. The pleasure came quickly and I let myself moan, knowing that's what he wanted to hear.

This one wasn't like the man I had been able to see. He didn't waste time asking me questions; he kept things as short, sweet and powerful as the fast strokes he was making over my clit, making the oversensitive nerves protest. "Do you want me to fuck you, slut?"

"Yes, Officer," Damn that cop with his quick hands. I had fully intended on going into this as a mouthy miscreant. It hadn't worked out as smoothly as I had planned.

"Is that supposed to be this begging I'm hearing so much about?" he said, partly to me and partly to the other man. He completely pulled away. I could hear footsteps as my heart pounded, thinking he was walking away.

"No! Wait, please. Please, Sir, don't leave. Please fuck me!" I tried to spread my legs as wide as I could in those damned heels, feeling more sweat form across my body despite the cool air of the night. I couldn't believe how pathetic I was being, but it surprised me even more that I was loving every minute of it.

I heard him snicker and walk forward. He hadn't gotten nearly as far away as I'd thought. He unzipped his pants quickly and grabbed me by the hips, pulling me off of the sofa. He grunted angrily when I stumbled in my heels, bent over and pulled them off my feet quickly. Nervousness twisted my stomach as I remembered the idiotic complexity that the shoes involved. He got them off quicker than I expected, giving me the impression he must've done this before. Grabbing my hips again, he let go to angle himself before he pushed hard into me. Without letting me adjust he started to fuck me quickly, holding me as steady as he could, pushing in and pulling out. Just as I let a moan of surprise pass my lips, I felt something warm trail past them and over my cheek.

"You're going to suck my cock, you filthy cunt," the first cop said, "and you're not going to swallow a single fucking drop until you've earned it."

I felt myself tighten at the words, making the man behind me groan slightly.

"Ah, fuck she is tight," he said through harsh breaths.

I felt a small slap of skin across my face, realizing that he must've hit me with his cock for not responding. I felt myself turn red at how ridiculous I must have looked. "Yes, Officer," I said clearly, "I will."

I felt the soft skin cross my lips again, and I opened my mouth, wrapping my lips around my teeth quickly, as he pushed past them. I felt a hand pulling my hair, and his cock moved in and out of my mouth, leaking slightly salty but sweet drops of precome everywhere. I licked as much as I could, feeling pleasure buzz through my vulva when he groaned in approval. It was hard to focus on moving my tongue and smelling the intensity of it all and the immense feeling of the other man fucking me roughly. I tried to block out the fucking as much as I could, letting moans pass my lips when they got the best of me. He tightened his grip on my hair, making me worry I had made a mistake.

"Fuck her harder," he said between his breaths. "Make her moan more."

The other man reached around to finger through my labia, pushing his finger on my clit the same way he had done before. The nerves crackled in protest, but the feeling of his fingers moving so rapidly made me lose concentration on anything else. I missed the stinky couch I had rested on before as my knees grew weak, and I moaned louder than I expected.

I felt myself gagging when he forced himself deeper down my throat. He pushed his hips harder and grabbed more tightly on to my hair, then he pulled out of my mouth sharply, and I could hear him moving his fist up and down on his cock.

"Hold your mouth open, slut." I did as he said without hesitation, sticking my tongue out as far as I could. I hated the black blindfold that prevented me from seeing his face. The muscles in my lower back ached as I held myself still. The harder I breathed, the drier my mouth became. I wanted to wet it again, but I didn't dare close it.

He shoved the head of his cock into my mouth again, knuckles bumping my check frequently as he began to breathe sharply. I closed my mouth around it, feeling the moisture return.

"Do you want this, whore? Do you like this?"

My pussy was starting to burn from the fingers grazing my clit and rubbing my labia. It wasn't a bad burning, like that of a paper cut or a knee after a particularly rough fall. It was sweet, magnetic, ragged and thorough, and as it intensified, I began to forget about everything.

The hand pulled away from my clit, and a harsh slap to my ass pulled me farther from the burning and made me instinctively tighten. The man behind me groaned just audibly.

"Answer when I speak to you," I heard from in front of me. "And keep your mouth where it is," he added, under his breath, through a few groans of his own.

I tried to form the word *yes* with his cock in my mouth, but it didn't come out sounding like anything but a grunt. I felt slightly ridiculous, but the burning began to slowly return. "Yes, what?" he growled.

For a second my mind was blank. Inwardly, I cursed, hoping the man fucking me would slow down a little so I could collect my thoughts. A second slap stung my ass. He pulled his cock from my mouth, grazing just the tip over my lips. From his short breaths, I knew what he was about to do. The burning started to kick in further, and I whimpered.

"If you can't be bothered to address me properly, slut, you don't deserve to swallow."

The man behind me ceased thrusting suddenly, causing the burning feeling to plateau. It felt good having him in me, but it didn't do any good unless he moved. I heard his breaths coming shorter, and I wanted to tear off my blindfold. Now that I could think, I combed my head for the proper way to address him. Just as the idea popped in, I felt warmth falling down my lips and smearing my chin and cheeks, and I felt my pussy clench lightly. He spread the warmth across my face everywhere but inside my mouth as he caught his breath. The man behind me pulled out and pushed in again, grabbing my hips harshly and resuming a quicker pace. The burning came back almost instantly, making me moan loudly. The other man still had my chin cupped in his hand, fingering the drying come on my face.

"You moan so well," he said through what I knew was a smile. "You've had a lot of practice, haven't you? Tell me...do you come as well as you moan?" He pulled my chin up a little higher, leaning to whisper in my ear. "Are you going to come for me? Are you going to be a good little slut for me?"

Without giving it a second thought, I muttered, "Yes, Officer."

I could feel fingers slipping down toward my clit again, and I knew it was over.

"Good little slut. Come for me then."

The burning intensified sharply, running from my clit up through my body, coming out of my mouth without a sound. I heard the man behind me groan loudly as my pussy clenched forcibly. I held my breath, concentrating on the echoes of pleasure vibrating through my body like the deep bass of a loudspeaker. The man behind me pulled out while the man in front of me murmured, "Good little slut, come for me," making my pussy clinch even harder.

After a few moments, I was roughly draped across the arm of the couch nearby, as loose as a rag doll. Hands pulled my hips and pushed my legs open as I leaned over the couch's arm. My pussy was still flinching as I breathed, an entirely different burning covering my labia, making blood pump through my clitoris so harshly that I could have sworn I felt my heartbeat right there.

"Look at that," the man who'd come on my face said, "How much do you think that's worth?"

Fingers traced my sensitive labia, pushing inside of me. I felt completely malleable and soft. "A lot," the other man uttered. The fingers left and I felt nothing but the cool air mingling with the wetness that coated my labia. "I think we should take her back to the station and see how the rest of the boys like her."

SEALSKIN

Kirsty Logan

Another sleepless night watching the moon crawl across the sky. I turn in bed, flip the pillow to the cool side, tug some of the covers back from my husband's sleeping grip. Nothing works. The moon slipping in around the blinds lights the room like an old black-and-white film, everything dark with silvered edges. Rory's snores sound like a grumbling bear. Every time I start to drift off they change rhythm, snapping me awake again.

There's a feeling deep in my belly that won't go away, making the heat between my legs pulse regularly with the beat of my heart. I could slide myself toward Rory, climb on top of his sleeping warmth, slip him inside me and ride myself to the tipping point of pleasure before he'd even properly awoken. I think about his drowsy hands stroking my hips, his sleepy kisses. I turn the pillow over again and sigh.

There's no use lying here with my eyes wide open.

I slip out of bed and into my dressing gown. Padding downstairs, I'm conscious of just how quiet it is here on the island.

After twenty years in the middle of London, the Isle of Skye is so quiet it deafens me. I fill the kettle with water, switch it on, switch it off again. I don't want anything. No; I do want something, I just don't know what it is.

From upstairs, Rory's snores are muted but still audible. I tap my bare feet on the kitchen floor and look at all the things I do not want. If I hold my breath, I can hear the shush of the sea. I slip my feet into the Wellington boots by the back door, pull on Rory's waterproof jacket and slip down the garden path. The sea is spread out before me, heavy as black velvet under the darkened sky. The summer air is cool enough to make me pull the jacket tight around me, and it brings up goose bumps on my legs where the breeze slips between the coat and boots. It makes my heart beat harder, as if the wind is the fingers of a dozen strangers against my skin.

I step carefully down the path to the beach. Our cottage is perched neatly on the edge of a cliff, not close enough to be at risk of high waves but close enough for walking on the beach whenever we please. I stumble on loose pebbles strewn across the path and have to jump the last few steps onto the shore. The sky, the sea, the sand under my feet: everything out here is dark and soft and quiet. I plant my boots wide apart and stare out to sea. I feel like I am the only person on the entire island. I hear the steady hush of the waves and smell the salt in the air. The moon winks at me from behind a cloud. Breathing deep, I finally feel calm.

I turn to climb back up to the cottage, back to bed and Rory's warm body, when I see movement farther down the beach. Immediately my heart starts thumping against my lungs and my tongue feels too big for my mouth. I'm standing on a deserted beach wearing only a too-big waterproof jacket and a pair of Wellies to preserve my modesty. I turn to run back up the path, then I realize what I'm seeing and stop.

Two women with skin as gray as a raincloud are entwined in the sand. They are aware of nothing except one another; certainly not my staring eyes and pounding heart. I take a step closer. Their bodies are as slim and rounded as seals. I can hear the gentle moans from their throats, and I can feel the way their skin feels, sleek and soft against the sand. I can taste the salty heat of their bodies. I can feel every sensation that they can feel, every caress and kiss, every flicker of pleasure. The heat between my legs intensifies, sending warm shivers from my clitoris to my throat, and I close my eyes and let orgasm overtake me.

The next thing I know, I'm in my bed with the late-morning sun burning hot in my face and Rory stumbling into his trousers. I lie back against the pillows, unsure whether I got up last night, unsure how time stretched and contracted in those predawn hours. Everything feels too bright and too loud, and I long for the soft gray sand of last night, the curves and moans of the women on the beach, the throb of my orgasm.... *No,* I think; *that was just a dream. It must have been.*

Downstairs I sip coffee and look out at the sea, making a mental checklist of things to do. Put the washing on, do the dishes, buy groceries, job hunt. It's been three months since we arrived on Skye, and "job hunt" has been on my To Do list every day since then. Rory was fine; mechanics are needed everywhere and he got a job in days.

But there's not much call for events organizers on an island with only a few thousand people. I've been turned down for work as a waitress in a seafood restaurant, secretary at a golf range, and ticket-seller for boat tours. I'd thought my long red hair and blue eyes would go down well in public service here, but apparently my London accent doesn't sound very pretty to the residents of Skye.

"Any plans for today, love?" asks Rory as he fills his flask with coffee.

"Just the usual."

"I know it's a bit shit just now, but you'll find something. There's not a lot out there. It's only a small island."

"It's been months. I'm getting bored of waiting around."

Rory kisses me on the top of my head. "I know, love. I'll bring you some paperwork home, that'll cheer you up."

I swipe a play-kick at his retreating rear end. He chuckles and pulls me in for a hug; I smell clean skin and a hint of oil from his work clothes.

I finish my coffee, kiss Rory good-bye, walk him to his car for another kiss then come back inside and decide which chore to do first. The ticking of the clock is irritating me and making me feel restless. The housework is waiting, but it will still be there after I spend a few hours having a nice long bath. And if I feel like a little self-love while I'm there, all the better for my motivation. I get my favorite bath oils, turn on the hot water and think about the girls on the sand.

By the time Rory gets home from work, all I've managed to do is masturbate twice, wash a few plates and confirm that there are no new job postings since yesterday.

"Pasta and cheese for dinner?" I ask as he hangs up his jacket.

"I know you so well." He pulls a plastic-wrapped block of cheddar out of his jacket pocket, puts it in my hand and kisses me.

Two hours later, we're cuddled on the couch, full of cheese and wine.

On the television, a man is investigating some sort of crime with the aid of several outlandish forensic techniques. I snuggle in under the weight of Rory's arm, putting my feet up next to his on the footstool.

The girls from the beach flicker through my brain: slick pale skin and whispers floating across the sand.

"Hey, Rory." I tilt my head up and press my lips in a kiss on the underneath of his chin.

"Mmm," he says.

"Do you think you might feel like…" (I recall the girls' soft skin, the throb of my orgasm, my heels pressing into the sand, and oh, how I want him inside me), "…uh…like some ice cream? I've got a craving."

"Sure. I'll get it." Rory ambles off to the kitchen, and I lean my head back against the couch. I appear to have forgotten how to seduce my own husband. We've only had sex twice in the three months since we moved here, and I'm not even sure why. I've desired Rory since the moment I pushed in front of him at a crowded bar: his broad shoulders, his dark blond hair, the way there's always a smile caught in the corners of his mouth. I took him home that night, and we've barely spent a dawn apart since. I don't even know how many hours I've spent pressing my skin against his, sliding up his body to dab kisses along his jaw, pressing my breasts against his chest and feeling his hardness against my lower belly. We could spend the whole night like that, enjoying each other's bodies, climbing slowly to orgasm after orgasm.

Lately, though, it just hasn't been happening. There's something about this island; I feel foreign here, uncomfortable, like I don't know how to find my way home. I want to love Rory again, but I've forgotten how.

Another night of watching the moon, turning over in my restless bed, and glancing jealously at Rory's sleeping shape. Every one of my breaths comes out as a sigh. My clitoris feels swollen and my heart is thumping too fast. I throw the covers off and pad downstairs, pulling on Rory's waterproof jacket and Wellington boots. The night sounds of distant birds and the whispering sea press tight around me. I can smell salt on the cool air.

Before I realize where I'm going, I'm on the path down to the sand. It must still be hours before dawn, and I am the only person on the vast silver shard of the beach. Lit up by the moon, everything looks two-dimensional, like paper cutouts. A thought slips across my mind: perhaps I fell asleep in bed after all. Perhaps none of this is real.

I step into the water, feeling the heat from my body emanate out into the night air, letting the water lap over my booted feet. Every wave sends tiny shudders up my legs and into my cunt. I feel like a kettle about to boil over. I walk down the beach, sloshing my feet in the shallow waves. I'm not looking for anything or anyone, I tell myself; there would be no one for me to see anyway. Images flicker behind my eyes of seal-smooth girl-flesh, of slippery salt-slick curves. Without thinking, I realize I'm searching for them. Ridiculous, I know; I probably dreamed them in the first place. Or maybe I'm dreaming now. But there! A movement on the sand. A twisting, fluid motion like bodies moving through water. I continue walking but keep my steps slow so that the waves do not splash too loudly.

It's the seal-women. Everything is the same as last night, except it's all about to change because now they see me. They beckon to me, their fingers impossibly long and slim, the moon reflecting off their skin.

I step closer. I feel like I'm not in control of my body; the heat from my clitoris seems to have boiled right up to the base of my throat. I'm dizzy and breathless and don't even know what the hell I'm doing here. But the girls are so close to me that I can see the dark lines of their eyelashes. They pull me to my knees on the sand and mirror my stance, stretching their bodies out so that their breasts rise high on their chests. I'm sure I was wearing clothes, sure I remember pulling on Rory's jacket and boots, but now all I feel is the warm grit of sand under my knees and the cool night air pulling at my nipples.

A cloud has passed over the moon and it's hard to see, but it looks like their skin is the soft gray color of the sky before rain.

Impossible, I know, but then it's impossible for me to be laid out on the sand with two strangers who are pressing their palms along my body, sliding their fingers across my nipples, slipping dual tongues toward the heat between my legs. My back arches with pleasure, and I dig my heels into the sand. I can feel every molecule of my body overflowing with joy, the boundaries of my body breaking like a dam.

This is my body, but I feel their bodies, too: I feel the touch of their hands at the same time as I know how they feel touching me. They are a part of me, and I am a part of them, and their loving me is me loving myself. Their tongues press up inside me together, and I shout the strength of my orgasm out across the beach.

Every moment of pressure and worry seeps out of my mind and scatters away among the sand. The waves tiptoe in and sweep it all away. I lie back on the sand and watch the women. They are walking away, hands held at hip-level, hair tangling in the breeze. I notice two piles of gray fabric on the nearby rocks, and the women pick up the fabric and slip it onto their bodies like they're diving into a pool. I must be confused because the fabric fits them like a second skin, but suddenly they're changing, their bodies filling out, transforming into rounded shapes with short arms and soft middles, and as the sea closes over them all I see is the retreating tails of two seals.

In our bedroom, Rory is sprawled across the bed like a starfish. His face is softened by sleep, and his mouth is slightly open so I can see the white edges of his bottom teeth. I slip under the covers and press my body full-length against his. He's not fully awake but already I feel him responding, his cock hardening against me. My body feels alive, every inch of my skin responding to his touch.

He starts to shift under me, spreading his hands over my hips and nuzzling into my neck. I scatter kisses along his hairline; he smells of warm skin and cut grass and shampoo.

"Hey, you okay?" he mumbles, finally coming awake.

"Yes," I say. "Yes. Everything is okay."

"What do you need?"

"Just this," I say. "Just you."

I slide down his body, swirling my tongue over his nipples and pressing my breasts against him. His gasp makes me smile. If my advances surprise him, he seems to be dealing with it very well. He's tangling his fingers in my hair and tugging gently on my earlobes, and I know what that means. I keep moving down his body until my mouth is right over his cock. In the darkness of the room I can see that the tip is gleaming, and it feels solid as a tree root in my hand. Slowly, slowly, I slide him into the O of my mouth. He makes a sound low in his throat and presses his body back against the bed. The hardness of him in my mouth is making my cunt throb harder, and all I can think about is the feeling when he comes inside me.

I spin my body around so that I'm positioned over his face, and then I lower myself. He presses his mouth against my cunt, his tongue flickering over my clit, and I can't help but let out a deep moan. I pull back a little: I feel so close to the edge that I'll orgasm within minutes, and I want us to come together.

In one smooth movement he lifts me, turns me and sits me down on his cock. I'm so wet that he slides right inside me. For a moment I can't move, so overwhelmed with that feeling of being filled, of my cunt stretching deliciously around him, of the tip of his cock pressing against just the right spot. He strokes his hand down the back of my neck, between my shoulder blades to the small of my back, and by the time he gets there I've started to move on him, rocking my body so I can feel him moving inside me. We're both gasping, calling out names and words, deaf to everything except the movement of our bodies together.

Stars flash behind my eyes and the whole world shrinks to the size of our bed: his body, my body, and everything else is darkness. Orgasm explodes inside me, pressing the breath from my lungs and a shout from my throat. He holds me tight and comes inside me, the rhythmic throbbing setting off smaller orgasms in me. We shudder to the end of these feelings, scattering kisses. Then we lie back in bed, curled as close as clams on rocks and listen to the shush of the ocean.

OPPORTUNITY

Cynthia Hamilton

"Never?"

It was one of those unexpected natural lulls in conversation, and Anne's outburst carried clear across the bustling dining room. She leaned forward, cradling her beer in her hands like she was protecting it from the news and lowered her voice. "You've really never been with a guy?"

Lin cringed and slid down an inch in her seat, cheeks burning with what she hoped wasn't too obvious a blush. She lifted her glass to her lips, hiding behind a cooling sip. Anne wasn't one to back down, especially with a few in her, and the rest of her friends were watching her expectantly, too. She drained the last of her glass slowly, but soon there was no more wine to stall her reply. She glanced longingly toward the bottle but didn't reach for it. *Clearly, I've had too much already,* she thought.

Celia's hand, hidden by the tablecloth, slid over her thigh and gave her a steadying squeeze. "Hey, Anne. I hear you're moving in with Kate. When's the big day?"

* * *

Lin pulled her long, black hair into a ponytail, watching Celia's reflection come up behind hers in the bedroom mirror and slip gentle arms around her waist, snuggling close. Physically, they were a study in contrast, with Lin's slender frame and delicate Asian features set against Celia's tumble of bottle-red curls and generous curves, but that only made them a more striking couple. Lin secretly loved the way they turned heads wherever they went.

Celia nudged the strap of Lin's tank top down her arm and traced lazy kisses up her smooth shoulder. In the mirror, Lin watched her nipples harden to obvious peaks under the clingy gray fabric. She leaned back, tilting her head to offer up the side of her throat.

"Thanks for the rescue at dinner," she murmured, reaching back to Celia's hip with her reflection as a guide. The mirror only disoriented her; when she lifted her gaze back to Celia's lips, her fingers found skin instantly by feel.

Celia laughed quietly against her neck. "The look on Anne's face..." Her hands slipped up under the stretchy top, cupping Lin's modest breasts and kneading them until a moan rewarded her. Applying a bit of pressure at one, she turned the smaller woman toward the bed. They crossed the short distance together.

Under the soft, clean sheets, with the lights out, they found each other again with a lingering kiss. Lin hooked Celia's leg with hers to pull it smoothly between her thighs. The motion was practiced and graceful; a comfortable, familiar fit. "You seemed a little surprised, too."

Celia nudged the top up and closed her hand around Lin's breast again, pressing two fingers around her nipple and scissoring them with subtle shifts. "Well, it's just...we've never talked about it, but I figured you'd have experimented in college or something. Dated in high school before you came out…" She closed her fingers in a gradual pinch around the aroused peak until Lin gasped and her hips squirmed. Then she added, "I don't mind that you didn't, you know."

Lin mirrored the movement, curving her palm to Celia's heavy breast and kneading in supple retaliation. She rocked herself lightly against the leg she'd captured. "My parents didn't let any of us date, and then I went away to an all-girls' college. My first date was with a woman. Men just…weren't even in the picture." She slid her hand downward, following Celia's naked curves to her hip.

Celia squirmed her thigh more firmly between Lin's legs, pressing with a slow rhythm that matched the gentle knead of her hand. "Ever been curious? It's okay if you haven't. Just because I'm bi doesn't mean that I think everyone has to be."

Lin's lips parted. She could feel her own heat every time she pressed forward against Celia's thigh, and her whole breast was starting to tingle. She curled her fingers, drawing her short nails upward to make Celia shiver, and grinned when she got the result. Celia would know she was stalling, thinking, but with such a nice distraction, she doubted she'd mind. "Mmm. I guess I've always been curious, a little. But by the time I was at a point where I could do anything about it, it was like…where do I start? I don't know how to flirt with a guy, and all the ones I already know expect me to not be interested, and…" She hesitated, but Celia worked her black cotton panties aside, gliding bare touch along her smooth folds, drawing the confession from her lips. "And the porn I've read makes it all sound so, well, unpleasant."

Celia laughed softly in Lin's ear, following the sound with a suckling kiss at her lobe. "Unpleasant how?" Celia nudged her onto her back, fingers taking over where the pressure of the thigh left off.

Lin took a slow breath, fighting for her train of thought while a fingertip teased her own wetness up and around her clit. Her fingers closed on Celia's breast again, rolling the nipple until it was as hard as her own. "Mm. My roommate had this book... It was so extreme it wasn't even hot. All these men hung so huge they could barely fit inside, coming copious bucket-loads..." She trailed off for a moment, distracted by the building ache in her breast. "Mm. I don't know how much of that was true and how much was just male fantasy fulfillment, but it left me less than interested in finding out."

"It's really not like that at all." Celia trailed lazily up and down Lin's slit, a smooth rub that parted her glossy labia. "It feels thick..." One finger eased inside the snug heat of her sex, then disappeared only to make way for two a moment later. "And full... And hot." Lin's back arched and she let out a slow sigh. Celia turned her wrist, the slick sounds of Lin's arousal accompanying the smooth thrusts of her fingers now. Celia knew her well enough not to draw attention to the way the conversation was heating her up, and Lin was grateful.

"I would. Just once. Just to see," Lin breathed. Her hips rose to meet each plunge of fingers. "I'd never be able to look the guy in the eye, after..." Celia's thumb finally brushed her clit, and Lin's lips parted in a breathless gasp that melted to a teasing grin at the scene playing out in her mind. "Maybe I'd let you watch."

Celia rewarded her with a sultry laugh and a passionate kiss. Her fingers curled to flutter against that perfect spot inside while the heel of her hand gave Lin a firm surface to grind against. Lin gave herself over to the tingling wave washing through her sex, suckling with needy pulls at Celia's tongue as her body bucked and writhed. She came with a burst of stars behind her eyes.

When she eventually fell asleep, it was with Celia's hand still curled possessively over her slippery folds and her thighs closed just as possessively around it.

Friday was date night, and they often surprised each other in little ways. Making reservations here or there, or securing tickets to a show. "It's my turn this week," Celia had announced as she poured Wednesday's morning coffee.

The box waiting for Lin on the bed when she got home on Friday was new: white and plain, tied with an oversized black satin bow. Inside, she found white tissue paper patterned in gold print. Inside the folds of paper, she found something almost as gauzy.

The smooth glide of silk across her skin was Lin's guilty pleasure—one of them, anyway. Black lace highlighted slinky charcoal gray silk, barely long enough for decency. Built-in garters dangled from the hem, ready to attach to the shimmery lace-topped stockings folded below. The matching panties were strangely designed, almost shaped like a—no. *They're crotchless,* she realized, and the resultant tingle zipped straight down her spine to settle in behind her clit.

She swallowed hard, carefully stripped out of her suit, and wriggled into the silk. She slid the panties up her hips and adjusted the lace to frame her bare folds, rolled the stockings up her smooth, waxed legs and fastened the garters to pull the gown sleek and taut. She turned before the mirror a couple of times, surveying her front and then turning and peering over her shoulder at her back. The taut curves of her ass peeked out in a deliciously indecent way, framed perfectly by decadent lace trim. She padded back to the bed to put the box aside and noticed one more piece of the ensemble resting in the bottom.

It only took her a moment to recognize the faux-fur-lined

blindfold. Hard leather with a plush interior and eye rests scooped away for comfort, it had been a regular player in their lovemaking a while back. She sat on the bed with one leg tucked under her and slid the blindfold down over her eyes with fond nostalgia. With it settled in place, she could blink comfortably in the darkness. The abstract patterns that sparkled in her vision matched the sparkle of anticipation that fluttered in her belly.

Lin shifted the blindfold up to her forehead and got up several times, each time to do some nervous task and then settle back down again. First, it was to turn the lights down low and put her work clothes away. Then to light candles and turn the lights off entirely. Then to put on music—sexy, ambient music on random shuffle and repeat. At last, out of things to fidget over, she lowered the soft blindfold over her eyes with determination and reclined on the bed. She drifted in aroused meditation, so intent on focusing her hearing toward the sound of the front door opening and then shutting again that she almost didn't recognize it when it finally came.

Now she was wide awake, heart pounding loudly in her chest. Senses straining, she heard the fridge open and close, followed by the squeak of the old floorboards in the hall. The bedroom door swished open, bare feet moved, and then the door closed again. Silence.

The scent of berries reached her. Fresh cut and sharply sweet and followed by the confirming quiet thud of a bowl set down on the nightstand. A metal bowl, Lin thought absently, not a glass one. There were other scents, too, but they were harder to place behind the fruit and the warm cinnamon of the candles. She smiled when she felt the weight of a knee on the mattress. She tilted her chin up and parted her lips, expecting the cool, tart kiss of a strawberry.

The lips that pressed to Lin's were warm, soft and familiar. Celia's curls brushed her cheek and Lin smiled, arching up to return the kiss with all her pent-up passion. Fingertips grazed over the silk covering one of Lin's hard nipples, and she moaned softly into Celia's mouth. "There's one more gift. If you don't like it," Celia whispered at her lips between kisses, "you can tell me. It's okay. But I think you will."

The hand traveled down over Lin's small breasts, between them and across the flat plain of her stomach, heading down. When they reached the damp, smooth crux of her spread thighs and trailed between the split lace of the panties, she heard a heavy breath. A breath not against her lips.

Lin started, but the comforting touch at her cheek and the warmth of Celia's lips on hers soothed her. Celia's breast was a heavy, familiar weight against her arm. "Shhhh. It's okay." Then her voice took that sly tone that always made Lin weak in the knees. "You said you wouldn't be able to look him in the eye, right? Well…"

The wave of heat between Lin's thighs flooded the back of her skull now. Blood rushing to her head, she thought, or maybe away from it. Her nipples ached. There was someone else in her bedroom. In her and Celia's bedroom. A man.

Strong, thick fingers rubbed her own gloss up and down over her labia. Now, on her naked skin, she could tell that they weren't Celia's fingers at all. A man was looking at her nether lips, flushed dark with arousal. He was watching her hips rock uncontrollably from the tingle of need blossoming through her core. The fact that he was causing those feelings, was touching her, was beyond her for now. Her mind reeled with it—with shyness, but that was only in the background; with amazement, more, and potential, possibility.

"Do I know him?" Lin whispered back. She caught Celia's

lower lip for a hard, suckling pull to show her approval; a moment later, a finger circled wet, slow pressure around her clit. Her kiss turned inarticulate and she moaned, slumping back down against the pillow. Her abdominals tensed, her pelvis pushing up toward the touch, seeking more.

"Does it matter?" Celia answered, then tapped a chastising finger to Lin's lips. It was slick, but with Celia's essence, not her own. Lin swirled her tongue around it greedily, pulling it into her mouth and shook her head without letting go. Then Celia asked, "How do you feel?"

She had to release the finger to answer. It wasn't fair, and she whimpered. The hand at her glistening cunt took the whimper as encouragement. A finger slid easily inside her, filling her with warmth, while something else—the thumb, she supposed?—still circled her throbbing clit. Her parted lips were slow to move in speech; Celia traced them, teasing them. "Dizzy," Lin whispered finally. A second finger joined the first and her back arched involuntarily, betraying her ecstasy. There was no way to play it cool and casual. And why should she? A fantasy come true was something to savor, and the lover selfless and devious enough to set it up was someone to reward enthusiastically. The opportunity to try this out, with full support and in complete safety…
"You'll stay?"

"I'll stay," Celia promised, shifting forward on the bed. Her chuckle was low and sultry. "Like I'd miss this show, *mi linda?* You should see how you're squirming."

Lin wet her lips, tasting hints of Celia's flavor. It emboldened her, like the wine had. "I want it." It was hard to make the breathy words pass her lips, but once they were hanging in the air—once she heard her own voice say them out loud and make them real—it was easier. "I want everything."

Lin clenched up inside, squeezing her silken passage around

his fingers in an intimate hug of encouragement. The next moan wasn't hers. Gentle pressure nudged her thighs apart, strong fingers spread her smooth petals, and a sudden whisper of breath slid coolly over the damp, heated flesh between her thighs. She raised her knees up and apart—all the invitation he needed.

His lips were strong and purposeful, and so was his tongue. He lapped a broad, warm stroke over her clit and continued with the point of his tongue up to the boundary of lace, then started back at his fingers, still thrusting smoothly inside her and licked upward again. The digits curled, scissoring and stroking over the spongy pad of her G-spot, and her reflexive arch slid her clit right up against his waiting mouth. She could feel the stubble on his cheeks and chin, faint prickling that mingled surprisingly well with the sharp tingling already building in her. Now the fingers were thrusting more powerfully, and he suckled with increasing fervor, devouring her. The sounds of her own wetness reached her ears, but she ignored the warm burn that rose to her cheeks. He pulled her clit into his mouth, bathed it with circles and flutters and direct presses of his tongue, refusing to be parted from it even as she squirmed beneath him. A hand closed on her breast, finding her nipple and pulling it outward with a firm pinch—Celia's trick, her touch. She could feel Celia's breath hot and ragged across her cheek, but she didn't feel the additional movements that would hint that her lover was pleasuring herself. No, she was just watching. Savoring.

His fingers curled up against that spot again and Lin bucked, a feral cry escaping her lips. Stars burst in the abstract darkness, but she barely noticed them for the stars bursting behind her clit and deep in her core. Those pulses of inner muscle were involuntary now, seizing up inside her and sending wave after wave of pleasure through her cunt. Slowly, he eased her down, slowing gradually before he stopped. Wet lips disengaged and kissed the peak of her mons, then her thigh. Fingers slid out, leaving her empty and spread, craving more.

He shifted between her legs, stroking up her thighs, up her sides, cupping her breasts and squeezing Celia's hand to her. He was strong, but he knew his own strength. And the whole time he'd been making love to her with his tongue, she realized, she'd forgotten to give a thought to who he might be.

There was a sound of plastic flexing, then of rustling, and his weight shifted from knee to knee. And then warmth returned to her cunt before she could think about it further. A thick presence painted her slickness up and down her parted labia, then angled just right and started to press inside her. Warmth. God, he was warm. Even through the thin layer of latex separating his cock from her, she could feel the heat of his body. Still awash in sensation from her climax, she was certain she could feel every ridge and vein.

Celia's strap-on didn't see as much action as the blindfold had. It came out of the toy drawer on occasion, but it wasn't their favorite. Lin didn't like using it because she couldn't feel Celia reacting inside if she was using a toy rather than her own body, and besides, she thought she looked more comical than sexy with a big purple dick dangling around and bumping off her thighs. She didn't mind receiving it, but there again, it was frustrating to know that Celia couldn't feel how wet she was or the way she'd squeeze her muscles down encouragingly inside. Still, Lin had assumed that the experience of having a lover between her thighs, slowly filling her with the thickness of a phallus, was a fairly standard one—whether the phallus happened to be attached biologically to the lover or not.

She'd been so wrong. The toys had never felt this warm, this pliant, this...alive. It was the same and yet completely different. As he rocked forward with a heated groan and sheathed his cock inside her, spreading her snug passage around him and pressing the firm, solid weight of his hips down against her pubic bone, she tensed again. She couldn't tell whether the pulsing waves inside her were aftershocks or a new climax crashing on the heels of the first.

He flexed his body in a smooth, hot grind then rested in her for a few moments, reveling in her molten heat just as she reveled in the way his cock conformed to the subtle curve of her body. She moved her hips, feeling it glide thick and hard against her upper wall. The press of his groin against her clit was unyielding and warm, perfect to grind up against.

Her movement spurred his. Shifting up to his knees and cupping his hands firmly under her ass, he started to thrust, dragging the length of his erection back and forth, filling and stroking her. The gown pulled on the stockings and the stockings pulled on the gown, shifting waves of taut silk creating a constant awareness of her breasts, as if smooth fingers fluttered just over her nipples. Every grind and undulation of her body renewed their hard, needy ache.

Celia's presence left her side, but only for a moment. Lin felt the mattress bow on one side of her head, held very still so that the knee swinging across wouldn't clock her in the face, and she took a deep breath of her lover's aroused scent. She heard additional sounds of wetness: kissing. She smiled and craned her neck upward and found one of Celia's plump folds. Capturing it in her lips, she used a pull of suction to urge the slippery petals down to her.

Celia lowered the rest of the way. Lin pressed her lips firmly around the swollen little pearl and bathed it with her tongue, then delivered an intimate tongue-filled kiss right to her lover's core. Now gasps, quiet moans and slick wet sounds filled the room completely. She could only hear and imagine the meeting of mouths above her, but she felt every stroke of the man's thick cock driving into her and heard her own arousal in the humid slap of each thrust. He was heating up now, faltering in his rising rhythm, and she almost thought she could feel him swelling even harder inside her.

Celia rocked firmly on her face until all Lin could do was keep her tongue extended or her lips pursed while her lover guided her clit, taking what she needed. Her squirms dislodged the blindfold, and Lin opened her eyes without thinking. Glistening candlelit folds moved above her, familiar ample curves beyond them. Her fingers tightened on Celia's thighs, and she closed her eyes again. The man pushed Lin's thighs back toward her body, fucking her at a steeper, tighter angle. A new wash of tingling pleasure blossomed through her. She could feel it pooling in her, building. She clenched down on the cock and was rewarded with a strangled, needy cry and feverish, pistoning plunges. He was as close as she was.

Kisses grew fierce and frantic above her. Her tongue stabbed upward, squirming into Celia's narrow entrance. Celia's folds slid back and forth across her slick lips with the quick jerking dance that announced her climax. Lin dug her fingers in harder and a husky feminine groan was her reward.

The man grunted and drove deep, grinding her on the root of his cock and brushing her pulsing cervix with his tip. Ecstasy bubbled up inside her. When she gave herself over to it, it burst like a shaken champagne bottle with unexpected force. Waves of heat pulsed through her, and the spasms deep in her sex now weren't voluntary ones. Hard, rhythmic, her climax thumped just out of sync with her pounding heartbeat. Then she heard his explosive groan and felt the answering pulse twitching through her, and she knew his pleasure had peaked as well. The condom between them was filling with his seed, a little more for every involuntary jerk of his hips. She relaxed in his grasp, turning her head to rest her lips against Celia's thigh.

When she found control of her limbs again, she reached up and nudged the blindfold back into place with a sated smile.

Rounds of fevered fucking had been interspersed with quiet snuggling and slow, languid kisses that had, inevitably, led back to more. He didn't leave until Lin had sampled everything she wanted to try—everything but the berries, completely forgotten on the nightstand. Celia brought the bowl to Lin in the tub, feeding her a piece of fruit and joining her in the sea of warmth and bubbles. Lin knew the dreamy smile was still stuck on her face.

"What'd you think?"

Lin pulled Celia back against her and slid her arms around her lover's beautiful curves. "Thank you so much for that. It was something I never thought I'd feel. It was...mm. So intense."

Celia shifted a little and turned to her, studying her eyes. There'd been something in her voice, and she knew Celia had caught it. "But?"

Lin smiled. She touched a strawberry to Celia's nose. "But he wasn't you."

LAPS

Sommer Marsden

I can see him there as I round the curve—Gus—like a wraith, like a malicious spirit. I swear I can see his white-white smile in the purple twilight air. I'm probably hallucinating. I snap a fingertip length off the twig, and I drop it on the ground. One more lap down.

"You can walk this one," he says, so softly I think maybe I imagined it. But I nearly weep with gratitude. I walk—a fast pace for anyone—but fuck, it's walking not running, and that's all that matters.

My heart pounds and my ears buzz, and I feel like with my next breath I could pass out, be sick or maybe just expire entirely. The soft early evening breeze pushes Gus's laugh across the air to my ears. I shiver.

I walk as fast as a human can and worry at my stick with my fingertip. I'm not sure when I started that ritual. Maybe the first time Gus brought me here to train, rewarding me afterward. He punished me hard, making me run until my body was so out of control I shook with the force of my anxiety. But when my galloping heart slowed to a pound and my eyes regulated themselves so the bright spots disappeared from my vision, he gave me my just rewards. And I was hooked.

I rub at the stick like a string of worry beads, rounding the corner of the track where he stands. My stomach sizzles with nerves and I feel lightheaded. What will the verdict be? I snap off a tiny section of the stick and drop it. It is my way of tracking laps, of passing time, of delivering my own bit of punishment to a dried-out twig from a majestic tree.

"Run and then walk and then run this one. So one third of running, one of walking and that last third, baby, you better haul ass," he says, his voice harsh and dark.

I run. I picture—to pass the time as I mete out punishment to my own struggling body—his fingers coming at me. Cool with dark paint. Gentle due to my hard, hard work. I picture him laying me flat in a bed of black and taking me there under the skies that soar like black velvet domes with pinpricks of starlight for accent. I picture Gus, flipping me, bowing me low, ramming into me from behind and fucking me until the only light in my world is the bright strobe of my own emotion behind my closed eyelids.

I feel the telltale slide of moisture in my sports panties that is most definitely not sweat. I feel the subtle kiss of my nylon running shorts on my bare legs that tempts me like an inanimate lover. I walk, forcing my elbows to fly high, my legs to stay true. And when I round the section where the announcer's platform sits, I start to run full out though my skin is tingling in that bizarre way that says I am flirting with the line of too much, too fast, too far.

I round the bend, my sneakers smacking the track with a vengeance. He is laughing. I can hear him. "Come on, Robbie.

Roberta Jean Monroe. Hustle. Make this count. This is mile five. Final lap. Slam it," he roars, and I take off like the devil himself is nipping at my heels.

I rub that stick so hard I expect it to catch fire. I'm desperate to go anywhere in my head that is not focused on my distraught body. I need to go to any mental place that allows me to find a Zen state. To find a way to push away the ache and throb in my left knee, the stitch in my right side. Any place that makes the unstable bang of my heart in my chest less frightening or blots out the hot cold war of my skin because it is struggling to cool me despite the calm, gentle breeze of the May evening.

I am desperate and I run, proving myself to me, to him, to anyone watching. And when I have proven myself, Gus will prove what a good girl I am. That is my reward and I push my mind to find that place in my head, that place where Gus is showing me that I am his good, good girl.

Before I know it, my sneakers trip past that final white line and Gus whispers, in the now near-dark, "Walk it off, Robbie."

I drop my beloved stick. Stagger past him for one more lap, letting my discordant body find its rhythm again.

When I come to pass him again, he is standing on the lip of the grass where the high school kids play football on Sunday; where someone has put a few spectators' benches—I can only assume so that watchers can get an up close and personal view of folks abusing themselves for the sake of health. I laugh out loud and Gus smiles. I can barely see the flash of his grin in the navy blue night.

"If you'll report to the long jump arena, we'll take care of business," he says in a faux announcer's voice, but his words are dark and gruff and I can hear the want in them now.

He is always the most eager to get at me when I have been pushed past the point of reasonable pushing. I wonder again why I ever took up running. I wonder yet again why I ever told Gus. But I know deep down—because my stomach has curled in on itself and my cunt has double clutched around nothing but a memory—that Gus is about to remind me.

My feet are heavy but my insides feel floaty as I hurry to the sandpit for the long jump. The sand sucks at my sneakers and whispers with each step. I hear Gus's belt buckle in the dark—first the merry jingle and then the sound of his zipper.

"Shuck the clothes. Get down on your hands and knees, Robbie," he says, his voice a lick and a murmur in the blackness.

After kicking off my shoes and my footie socks, I drop my shorts and my panties, my running top and jog bra. The cool night air kisses me between the legs and under my arms. It runs a cold tongue of air under my breasts where I am hot and sweaty. My skin revolts with a legion of goose bumps, and when Gus reaches out in the dark to paint me with eye black—the black cream that football players use to ward off the sun—I whimper. He'll make me as dark as the night and then he'll fuck me. Out in the open, but invisible to see.

I once asked him why he doesn't paint himself, and he laughed. "I'm a chameleon. If I don't want you to see me, you won't. Not like you, Robbie. All of you simply screams look at me!" From my long strawberry blonde curls to my big blue-green ocean water eyes, he says I must be looked at.

I drop to my knees and the sand says *whump* softly under me. Gus kneels to paint my face, with large swooping touches of his big gruff fingers, under my eyes, down the ridge of my nose, over my cheekbones. I feel like my eyes must be glowing—as if I'm some luminescent sea creature who creates her own lamplight at great depths. He smiles at me, his fly sagging open. I can see his erection pressed to his boxers. He knows where my head has gone.

"If you're going to fly on that track like some bird of prey, some fast-moving underwater sea nymph, some force of nature, you should be camouflaged like one, yes?"

I nod and nearly purr as he paints the black paint along my shoulders and between my breasts, pinching my nipples so I shake. He runs a hand over my flanks, my back, my ass, smacking so my body zings with shock. Gus is not really painting me now, there is too little in that tiny pot. But he is speckling me like a jungle creature, and I tremble under his warm, calloused hands. Then he pushes his fingers deep into my pussy and I go still. I freeze, on hands and knees, heart escalated back to where it was when I was running, beating like some evil war drum that's portent is death and blood and destruction.

"You did good," he says, pushing one wet finger into my ass so that I bite my bottom lip. I bite too hard and I taste the coppery tang of my own blood on my tongue.

I don't thank him. If I talk too much, he'll add more the next time. I hang my head and am humble—the way he likes, the way I prefer.

"First you make a spectacle of yourself. Laps and sprints, long tangle of hair flying. God, your face gets so red, Rob. Like you're going to go up in a ring of fire and smoke. Some fairy-tale witch burning on a pyre." He's taken himself in hand; I hear the hushed rustle of cotton and movement. His cock runs the length of my wet slit and he aligns himself to me, fingers sinking deep into the flesh of my hips. My muscles shake and quiver, already exhausted from being pushed. Now they are supporting me and he is sinking deep.

I gasp, bite my tongue, still tasting blood and the sour sweet flavor of a mouth dried and then rewet from running hard. I put my head down farther and my hair wallows in the sand.

"And now you're all painted up. As black as night. As dark

as that giant sky over us. No one can see you but you're out here in the middle of this track. In the middle of this field." He's moving now, slow and sure—even, measured thrusts that make me want to scream and beg him to do me faster, deeper, harder. But I wait. "And all around us a magic ring of homes. Little family homes, grouped around this center. Warm yellow kitchen windows glowing around us like feral eyes." His finger plunges back into my ass and he's pushing it deep, fucking me harder. The head of his cock is nudging that secret bouquet of nerves deep in my wet, ready cunt. One of his hands still anchors me with a biting grip on my hip bone.

"Yes," I say. These people have come to watch me run laps and sprint. I have run 5Ks and half marathons with some of them. They know me by sight, by name.

"Anyone could see. Not some heroine pounding the track with her tennis shoes. Not some runner pushing herself to achieve. But some painted, primal, fucked-up wild woman who's getting banged in the sandpit. All dirty and raw and—"

"Yes," I say. This is how you let go when your body and mind tell you that you have to be perfect. Good girl, pure girl, kind nice sweet girl next door girl... This is what you need. Right here. Smudged and dirty, sweaty and sandy, being fucked in a sandpit by a man who knows exactly how imperfect you want to be deep down.

"Breaking sticks and running from all the pressure." He knocks me flat then. Full on in the sand on my belly, his one hand worming under me so he can press the hot pad of his finger to my clit while he thrusts. He bangs into me—forcing me down and forward, getting deep, invoking friction because my legs are pinned under him, not much wider than my normal stance. And Gus presses that fingertip to my clit like he's tapping out Morse code.

dirty girl

bad girl

scared girl

my girl...

I hear that one outside my head because he says it. "My girl. My bad, dirty, struggling, running from everything, Robbie. My girl."

And I come. Shaking under him, sand in my hair, rubbing my clit raw, him pounding into me. I inhale fine grains, sputter but keep coming, the spasms in my cunt as sure and true as a charley horse or a shin splint. I come and he's pinning me, still moving until he bellows in my ear, his voice as rough as the sand, as black as the paint on my skin.

We lie there, facedown, filthy and grimy, hearts punching in our chests. Somewhere at one of the houses a radio plays loud country music. At another, a dog barks. Gus laughs softly and kisses the back of my ear. It sounds like a gunshot it's so loud.

"Come on. Let's get you home. Get you in the shower." He tugs up his jeans, buckles his belt, helps me step into my damp clothes.

When he kisses me, I clutch at him—to thank him, to feel his warm skin under my fingers. Gus runs his fingers through the tangled train wreck of my hair and says, "We'll come back. Day after tomorrow. I'm bumping you up to five and a half miles. Running, walking, sprints and whatever else I think of."

My brain jumps into gear. Five and a half miles—that's twenty-two laps. And at the end is...this. If I'm good. Twenty-two hard-core, balls-to-the-wall, whatever-he-says laps. I can do that.

ESPIONAGE

Rachel Kramer Bussel

You tuck your new pink and black coat, the one purchased earlier in the day just for this special evening, around your body, pull it tight like it's cold out, except you're indoors and the fire is roaring. You are cold, but it's the kind of cold that can't be heated by rubbing two sticks together or turning up the thermostat, the kind of cold that can only be vanquished once your heart catches up. Your heart is cautiously icy, watching and waiting; it isn't safe to let it melt just yet.

Instead, you look—you could say spy, except you have an invitation, an elaborate listing of reasons this will be the party to end all parties, delivered right to your inbox. You've been promised bubble baths, servants, champagne, s'mores, drugs, debauchery. Those things intrigue you, sure, since you're used to zoning out in front of the TV, quiet dinner parties, wholesome events like comedy shows and trivia nights, but you'd have shown up for gin rummy if it were held right here, in these rooms that hold a life that will never be yours, a life you've been given glimpses of but never truly peeked inside. Even better than any promise of party pampering, you've been granted access to this sacred space, this love shack you've up till now only imagined vividly. This is your chance to enter the inner sanctum, and you cling to it in the same way you hold your coat, and your heart—close. Still, despite the tacit permission, you feel like a spy, an Anaïs Nin emissary, as you walk through the rooms that make up their home, their urban house of love and lust and lasciviousness, a house you will never inhabit no matter how many times you fuck the master of it.

You've been invited here before, of course, when the lady of the manor was away; you don't quite know where she spent the night, and it doesn't really matter. Maybe she's a bed hopper, too. That night the coveted marital bed was yours for the taking, for an evening of borrowed, perhaps stolen, pleasure. It was so tempting, except the man you love would only be yours on temporary loan. Plus, you like the other beds you've christened with him, the beds that became yours with the ease of a credit card, the swipe of a key; the beds that are almost communally owned, yet allow you to feel like they are yours for the borrowed time they're allotted to you. You declined that chance to slip between his sheets, spending the night instead in a glamorous threesome with frosting and vodka, tonguing the one, bathing in the other, letting them take you away to something not quite an orgasm, not quite shameful enough to make you burn the way you need to, to come.

That burning, that fire that lights you up from the inside out, which turns pain into the most wicked of pleasure—he knows how to do that, the man of the house, the woman in the sheer black slip's husband. He knows exactly how to hold the match between his fat, meaty fingers, to strike it in such a way that the blaze erupts in one part of your body and spreads instantly to the rest. He can do it with a word, a whisper, a text, a hand, an image; the truth is, he can do it even when he's not doing anything at all. You only need conjure him in your mind and you're enflamed, a mixed blessing of desire and curse. He's told you he thinks about you when he puts on his belt, the one whose leather made you scream in Kentucky, whose buckle pressed against your throat in Montana, whose tip you kissed with sore, swollen lips in California. You've traveled so far to pretend he is yours, yet here, at ground zero, you realize just how mistaken you were; no matter how many states you undress in for him, she will always be there, wrapped around his ring finger, permanently embedded in his soul. On these trips, he tells you how he misses the scent of your vanilla perfume as you lie on those borrowed pillows; you in turn confess to miss the way he breathes deeply of your neck, like he's getting high off of it, snorting a line of euphoria directly to his brain. That is your ground zero: the smell, taste and touch of each other's body. Home has no place in your affair; instead it's a base you can claim in any state you find yourselves together in.

This home, certainly, is theirs through and through. You may be a guest or a spy; either way, you are an intruder, an outsider whose evidence will be wiped away after you step back outside. You feel his eyes follow you around the room, feel his palms sweat as you tilt your head back and let the journalist whose byline you've read countless times tilt your head against her breast and slide her red lipstick over your lips, painting them as if she were making love to you. In a way, maybe she is, her fingers crushing your jaw, the not-quite-liquid, not-quite-solid of the waxy ruby pressing hard against your lips, hard the way he used to crush them, hard the way you like it.

She laughs an almost evil laugh that makes you wonder what else she could do with the lipstick, and you feel a frisson of static pass from her small, bony hands into your cheeks when she pinches them, inspecting her work. You wonder, of course, if he's fucked her, even though it shouldn't really matter. Lots of things that shouldn't matter take up space in your mind, fragments of jealousy on permanent repeat. You pucker up just to give your lips something to do, someone to make contact with who is not him. Her tongue traces the red, teases, darts but doesn't claim you as her wicked laugh did. You let her know, with your lips, that she could have you, but she simply pulls back and smiles, her nails digging into your upper arm. Suddenly you want to pull her bleached-blonde hair, tug hard until she can't even make a sound, the feral domme inside of you flicking at your insides, aching to be let out for a moment. Instead you just smile widely and she slinks away to find another victim.

After, you think the lipstick will be smeared—that's only right, isn't it, after someone's just fucked you with a tube from MAC?—but instead, it's perfect. Redder than red, redder than you'd ever dare in your daily life. Fancy that. They should put that in an ad campaign. You go back to your spying-cum-ogling, your lips now signaling that you are the hussy you know yourself to be, the other woman come seeking vengeance, seeking something you will never have because it belongs to someone else.

Except that's not really how it is at all; you don't want what the woman in the slip has, the slip of a woman, the one whose body fits right up against his fleshy arm, whose presence you've felt like an erotic phantom from day one. You wouldn't trade your life for hers if given the chance, yet you can't help but hate her just a little and are surprised to find how quickly that hate snakes its way into your panties, ignites the chill that's been coursing through you since you stepped inside.

You watch her from across the room, laughing softly, nuzzling up against some sweet young thing. You could be the sweet young thing, you've been told—or warned. She wants to kiss you, he's let you know, a heads-up that only makes your head spin. You try to imagine what her body would feel like, what your fingers inside her would make her say, but you only get as far as her breasts in your mind. You already know what she tastes like, from that first date when he shoved his fingers into your mouth, fresh from the taxicab where he got his last feel of her until the morning. You watch her until it seems inappropriate to keep doing so, then look away, absorb the surroundings like you'll be writing a report on them later. This is likely your only chance, so you might as well make the most of it.

The apartment is nothing special in its layout, location, design; it's the decorations—the photo-booth strips, posters, mementos, bookshelves—that mark it indelibly as theirs. There's no centerpiece, no stunning work of art everyone gathers around; none of the other guests seem to be having an epiphany as they take in their surroundings, no one else is clamoring for more champagne with quite the edge of hungry anger that consumes you. The bubbles work much like a bubble bath, simmering, soothing, smoothing over any rough edges that threaten to erupt. You're glad you don't wear eye makeup because already the tears are swimming up, demanding release. You blink them back and look around for something—anything—to latch on to that does not remind you of traveling on a bus with sex toys stuffed in your bag so he could steal an afternoon away from her to shove them inside you.

People are stripping down for the promised bubble baths, sneaking off to corners and closets for make-out sessions, while you forage for more champagne. You will leave if you don't have it because you can only be here with those bubbles fizzing in your hand, *snap crackle pop,* like the cereal, before they provide a heat all their own to your insides. You find a bottle and clutch it to you, tuck it against your breasts, make people come to you for a fresh glass. He walks up, silently holds out his empty. You bite down, knowing that even MAC's finest won't withstand too many fresh, sharp bites, but not caring.

You pour, then watch him down the contents of his glass. His eyes meet yours and much as you want to look away, you don't. It'd be a lie to say you can't; rather, you don't want to, not really, not more than you want to look. You're sick of forbidden, stolen glances or unabashed stares as one member of an endless audience. You want to watch, but your eyes, like the rest of you, are greedy; they want to be the only ones watching, the only ones seeing precisely what you see. His eyes look back with that same greed, that look that makes you shiver because it seems to strip you bare.

You don't know what you want anymore, having been shaken and stirred so many times your essence has dissolved into something flat, your insides hollow as you take him in. When he grabs your hand you go, not even sure why, exactly. You squeeze yourselves into the closet and, finally, no one else exists—or at least, you are free to pretend in the dark that this is true. "I've missed you," he says and you want to cry for a second, the words too familiar from the countless times you've heard them whispered in your head. But you don't, not yet; there'll be plenty of time for that later.

You don't say a word for fear of saying too much. Instead you shut your eyes and wait; it's easier to offer your body when you don't know what's coming. His hand goes to your face; soft, sweaty fingers stroking your cheek, and you want to scream. It's too gentle, too tender. "Save that for your wife," you want to say but instead you turn your head to the side, to the wall, rub up against it like you wish you could rub up against him. He steps forward and his bulk is pressed against yours, surrounding you on all sides. He keeps going until you are flat against the wall. His hand claims your wrists, seemingly in one fell swoop, while his other hand reaches between your legs. He tears your black and gold fishnet stockings, the ones that cost twenty-eight dollars at Macy's, the ones so delicate you've walked with great care so as not to snag them, the ones that garner whistles and compliments on the street. The sound is loud in the quiet of the closet, and you know if your panties were as delicate they'd be in shreds by now too, but you're a basic white cotton kind of girl—at least when it comes to underwear.

His fat fingers find your wetness, a wetness that surprises even you. You didn't come here for this; you're supposed to be an observer, a spy, a detached spectator, not a participant. In the dark you can barely see a thing, can only feel. He wants his fingers to hurt, to hurt the way they used to, the way you used to like it, so your pussy is sore long after they're gone. He twists them and slams them deep inside you, and even though you're wet there, it does hurt in its way. He drops your wrists to press his hand against your cheek, to pin you in place, digits digging into the tender skin of your face, landing wherever they may.

You squirm and aren't sure if it's to get away or to get him in deeper. Actually, that's a lie; he's always known better than you what you want, a trait that's either the hottest thing ever or the apotheosis of infuriating. You push against him and instantly the mood changes; you are no longer simply star-crossed lovers reuniting, but something darker, deeper. You press hard with your hands, your hips, to fight him off—but not really. He pushes back with ease, his hand twisting your head into the wall, covering half your face. The harder he holds you there, the deeper the ache in your pussy. You try to twist to the side, give him an elbow blow, something to make him feel the impact, but he is more powerful than you by far. Even if he weren't, though, he would be winning, because this, finally, is what you've come here for: to struggle, to writhe, to argue with your body, to try to tell him, and yourself, that this is over, knowing all the while it will never be over, not really.

He knows you like to struggle, knows you like the adrenaline rush of giving your all to a wrestling match with a preordained outcome. If you were locked up, you'd be the type to rattle the cage. Instead, you silently provoke him, knowing he is getting harder by the moment, but for once, this is not about his cock. This is about you, about the tears now pouring down your face, about your decision to stay rather than flee. You hear the fluttery sounds of his wife laughing outside the door and this makes you growl. He presses you tight against the wall, firm behind you while his soft bulk is before you. What he wants, though, is not what you'd expected—it never is. He eases his hand off your face so you can take in some air, then rams four fingers into your mouth. "Get them nice and slick because I'm going to put this inside you."

You make a noise, a gargled moan, not sure how this will happen. He is forcing you, and yet he is not. You could call it off with a single, simple word, but it's one that's anything but safe. Safe would mean comfort, safe would mean calm, safe would mean something you've never been with him. You wouldn't dare use it here, and he knows it, knows that the power he wields is of the mind first, body second. The words have no sooner left his lips than you picture your pussy opening, stretching, hurting, for him. You can't let him know how much you want it, how much you like what he's doing; that would ruin the game, and the game is all you have.

You move to bring your leg up against him, thrust your knee somewhere it will make an impact, but he's on you in a flash. He whips something out of his pocket—a Swiss army knife.

Without opening it, he presses it to your lips, then holds your mouth open while he lets the metal touch your tongue. Despite yourself, you like it; you want it. You have no time to think, just then, about whether he uses it with her or all the other girls. You just let the tang enter your mouth, let all it represents remind you why you so desire him.

"Submit," he says, not a question but not completely a command, either. He knows you could keep struggling, keep moving, keep prolonging this teasing, taunting game. He knows it could get heated. He knows you could be in there far longer than propriety should allow. You can't move much but you let your eyes blaze at him for as long as you can before finally sinking almost imperceptibly against the wall. He gets it and eases off with the knife.

He could cut off all your clothes, and if he knew you had a second set stashed, he surely would, but instead he just lets the knife dance over your skin. He holds one hand over your mouth, lightly enough that you can breathe, but a reminder that he can take that away at a moment's notice. "On the floor," he says. It's dark, but you do it anyway. "You're going to take my fist, and you're going to like it." You get so wet when he says it you almost scream, your pussy contorting even as tears race to your eyes. You're back where you've always wanted to be, doing something for him—with him—that stretches your boundaries beyond all recognition.

You are no longer spying, of course; you've plunged right in, entered the enemy's territory. You are in her home, but if his hand is going to go inside you, you know you will be getting all of him for as long as that takes; fisting leaves no room for outside thoughts. Of course he has lube with him, and your heart twists the way your pussy does for that. He'd never really hurt you, he'd never be the guy going too rough, too fast, like so many others you've been with, unless he knew you were ready. "I bet you barely need this, since you're such a slut. I wish there were another guy here whose cock you could suck while I'm inside you." He says this while shoving your legs apart with his knees. "If we had a bed I'd tie your ankles to the bedposts and tape that pretty mouth shut. You'll just have to find a way to be quiet." He smears the lube against your pussy, then slaps it, hard, before pressing three fingers inside.

You are ready; so, so ready, and you take the three fingers in greedily, followed by a fourth. His other hand finds places to pinch you—inner thigh, belly—as you open for him, spreading your legs as far as you can, willing yourself to relax. You—the part of you that makes these decisions—want this, want this final time, this heat, this heaviness, but your body is more cautious, closing around his fingers as the thumb attempts entry. Your body, your cunt, knows he is almost too large to fit inside but you have overruled your body before, turning pain into the most dazzling of erotic highs. This is not like the times he's held you down and shoved his cock inside you, shocked you with the bluntness of it, making you play catch-up. He can't hurry this along. Instead he rotates his fingers and adds more lube and you grunt and bite your lip and feel him get a little farther inside.

He goes in and in and in, thumb curled up, and then there it is, the ball of his hand, this giant inside you. You've heard that the human heart is actually the size of a hand and wonder if, right now, he is giving you a part of his heart, a part that is only for you, a part you can treasure as you feel its outline pressing the tender, thin walls of your pussy wider and wider. The tears come—of fear, relief, pleasure, love—all at once, and you are grateful for the dark. He can hear them, that's fine, but seeing them is another story. Seeing them is a little too close for comfort. You lie there on the floor of the closet, stealing more than your seven minutes in a kinky kind of heaven, as his massive heart of a hand reels you in and lets you go. His other hand finds your clit, so hard and aching it could be a cock, and you think you'll hurt him when you come like that, squeezing so tight, the energy rushing all around, making your fingers tingle and your head so light it could float away. You see stars behind your eyes and have to drop your legs to the ground. His hand makes love to you, makes love appear inside of you even as you know this has to be the end. You want all of him, all the potential he has to love someone, and this is just a teaser.

"I'm going to pull out," he says after what could be three minutes or thirty. You want to protest, because once he's gone, the emptiness will be so huge you know that sex will never be enough to fill it. You reach for his wrist and he lets you take it, lets you half sit up and keep him there. There's a stillness to all this; a calm, Zenlike focus combined with the way it makes your pussy take over everything. You can feel him shaking, are sure he is sweating, and you take your fill of him, then lie back and let him leave. The silence is not deafening, but awe inspiring. You break it by leaning against his chest, listening to his heartbeat. You manage to block out all the noise outside the closet.

In a few minutes, you will emerge, splash some water on your face even though it'll ruin your makeup, take a sip of seltzer, and, unnoticed, quietly put on your soft, padded, pink and black coat amongst the chaos on all sides. You won't have it in you to say good-bye to the woman in the slip or the journalist, certainly not to him. You will ease out into the icy night and feel a rush of pride and power you didn't think he could possibly inspire. You will walk in heels the ten blocks to the subway and sit with your legs crossed as the heat he's left you with warms you from the inside out.

Before all that, he pulls you close, and you melt into him,

just a little. You are no longer on an espionage mission; there's no pretense of haughty glamour and detached coolness. You are just a girl listening to a man's heartbeat: *tick tick tick tock*. You let the rhythm lull you until your heavenly minutes are up.

ABIGAIL'S ICE CREAM

Janine Ashbless

The important thing to remember when making ice cream is to keep stirring the custard as it freezes; otherwise, the whole lot goes to icy lumps. When I first started making my own I used to churn the mix by hand, but these days I have it done by machines. Three or four batches can be on the go at once in the old dairy that now houses Abigail's Ices. Keep it moving: that's the trick. Break up those ice crystals as they form.

Turkish Delight: past and present combine upon the tongue as it melts. The taste recalls the sticky sweet bars eaten as a child, but up against that rears the dark and powerful chocolate of my adult palate, perfectly balancing the summer-garden nostalgia of the rosewater. I pick the pink rose petals myself and candy them before stirring them into the cream. Sweet and bitter, floral and earthy, light and dark, it is a glacé of sublime contradictions.

* * *

"I'm going to need some help getting the freezers out of the van," I tell the steward.

She looks down at her clipboard, frowning. "Did you give notice when you booked your pitch?"

"Yes—and I rang up last week to remind you. I spoke to a Mr. Addleman; he said there'd be no problem."

She snorts down her nose. "Well, he didn't write it down here. Still, we'll manage. I'll go find you someone to help." And she goes off, leaving me to haul the tent frame out of the van on my own and start putting it together. I think Mr. Addleman's going to get it in the neck. She looks like the sort who's used to telling everyone on the town council what he or she needs to do to be properly organized: she's wearing a tweed twinset on a summer's morning. It's all a bit like that today—a town fête writ large and run by optimistic amateurs who are slightly out of their depth. Not that I'm surprised. The fair marks the 360th anniversary of their castle's surrender to the parliamentary army and, well, that's not the sort of thing you practice every year.

I do a lot of shows in the summer months: agricultural shows (green Wellington boots, horsey women and hard-mouthed farmers); game fairs (guns and spaniels and camouflage trousers); craft exhibitions (well-off suburbanites). The one thing they all have in common is food. The punters want to eat. They want to try something different, a little luxury: spit-roasted pig and hot waffles and venison burgers...and Abigail's ice cream. Even at the Strawberry Fair in Cambridge, which is the tattooed alternative crowd and beer in plastic glasses and loud live music, I can easily shift two full freezer-loads on a hot afternoon.

Me? I'm actually a bit of an aging hippy-chick, though I try and hide the fact for some venues. Since Indian prints are finally back in fashion this year, today I'm wearing an embroidered, sleeveless dress I first bought when I was at college back in the Eighties (oh, no post-punk grunge for us: ours was a fine arts college). It still fits me, after twenty years and a child; there are some things I can be proud of. Its soft cotton swings with each turn, making me feel good about myself, and I don't think I'm out of place here. This particular fair is a combination of local celebration—they've got a historical reenactment group in: Roundheads and Cavaliers poking at each other with pikes—and charity stalls and family entertainment. It's an easygoing crowd and it looks like the sun's going to come out, which is great for my sales. It's going to be a doddle, if I can get someone to help me shift those freezers full of ice cream out of the van.

And then suddenly, as I'm working a tent pole into its canvas sleeve, there they are: two men standing over me, grinning. "Need a hand with that, love?" says one.

"Looks like a bit of a tight fit," adds the other with an audible smirk. "You need some K-Y, I reckon.'

I look up, acknowledging his teasing with a grin and a shake of my head. They're both wearing uniforms of some sort: green shirts and trousers, radios on their belts. Both strong-looking men, thank goodness, and in their twenties at a guess.

"We were told you needed a hand," says the one with the lube obsession. He's got a handsome square face and sun-blonded hair that would be curly if he let it grow any longer than his stubbly beard.

"Um." Standing, I look again at the NHS badges sewn on their shirtfronts. "From...doctors?"

He looks hurt. "Paramedics, love."

"Oh—right."

"We've got time to kill before the show kicks off," says the other, the one with the olive complexion and the dark nap of hair shaved so close that it looks like suede. "Mrs. Addleman asked if there was anyone available for some heavy lifting, so we volunteered."

Aha, I think. Mr. Addleman is doomed.

"Great, thank you. I've got two freezers full of ice cream in that van," is what I say. "They're on wheels but they're still really heavy. If you could shift them down into the stall area here…"

They get to it with enthusiasm. It turns out that the fair one is Matt and the dark one, Trev; that they've been stationed here with the ambulance all day to back up the St. John's first-aiders in case there's a serious incident, and that they're doing a demonstration in the main arena area later, helping the local fire brigade cut an "accident" victim out of his car. They're fit and chirpy and they josh each other and me. They insist on helping me put up the tent, and I can barely instruct them fast enough to keep up with their swiftness and confidence. In minutes the stall has taken shape. With a few casual blows of the mallet it's pegged securely to the ground. They connect up the freezers to the generator out back and get it started up for me with hardly any effort.

Oh, they make me feel old.

Vanilla: every ice-cream maker has to have some version of vanilla in his repertoire. Mine is Madagascan vanilla-pod and clotted Devonshire cream; the taste is rich and sweet and comforting. Even now when I make a batch it reminds me of bathing Skye when she was a baby, of talcing her skin and holding her tiny body to me. Vanilla is the scent of babies and breast milk. It's safe and infinitely satisfying, and it's what we all fall back on. It's my best-selling line. Plenty of people eat only vanilla.

"Bloody hell," says Matt. He's just spotted the price list I've hung at the front. "That's expensive ice cream!"

"Homemade, organic and fair-trade." I'm not abashed:

I'll cover my costs here on any reasonable day, but my profit margins are surprisingly slim and it's seasonal work. "I pick the fruit myself and make every tub. And the base is sheep's milk for most of them. That's not cheap."

"Sheep? You milk sheep?"

"Not me—I get it from a local farmer. He used to milk for the cheese trade, but he lost his contract and I stepped in to try turning it into ice cream. It's lovely stuff. Easier to digest than cow's milk too."

"Ginger and brandy snap," he muses. "Green basil. Strawberry and black pepper."

"Sounds good," says Trev. "Weird, mind; but good."

"Do you want some? I think I owe you both an ice cream, for this lot."

"You got double-choc-chip?" asks Matt, grinning.

"Brazilian chocolate and chili," I counter, daring him.

"Go on then. I can't resist a Brazilian." He winks; I roll my eyes in mock despair. But just as I open the freezer Trev's radio buzzes to life. I can't make out the words barked over the airways, but he switches in a second from affable to decisive.

"Gotta go. Sorry, Matt."

"No fair. I was hoping for a chocolate flake with that."

They hurry off at a jog. Matt looks back and shouts at me, waving his arm: "You owe us an ice cream! Don't forget!"

I wonder why I feel so warm and tingling inside, and why I was so disappointed when the call came through.

Sloe Gin: it's real sloes and real gin, though it takes some extra prep to make sure the alcohol doesn't make the ice cream slushy. Every winter when I reduce the syrup my kitchen fills with the scents of juniper and plum. I pick the sloes in autumn, cherishing each hard, steely purple fruit won from its barbed-wire twig. Then I prick them all over with a fork and bottle them in gin for months, until the liquor turns the color of rubies. I like gin, but too much makes me weepy; the sloes mitigate that. They are autumn's wergeld for the dying year, for the loss of summer. They are the compensation that comes with sorrow.

I'm lucky: the sunshine doesn't just win through, but rolls up the clouds and sends them packing. It turns into a lovely hot summer's day and by late lunchtime I'm selling steadily. So I'm in a bright mood.

But it's not just the sun and the trade; it's how the day started. It's ridiculous really, but Matt and Trev have really perked me up. Just the way they joked with me and looked at me, like it was more than a kindness they were doing and they were getting something out of my company; the spark in their eyes. Damn, but it's a long time since anyone but chivalrous old men flirted with me. I'm not used to it from guys younger than I am, and it's left me a little giddy. I have an extra smile for my customers today.

Oh, they were cute, both of them.

And, oh, I'm too old for this. They're young enough to be... okay, not really young enough to be my kids, but certainly not even a decade older than Skye, and she's still at university. I'm forty-two, for heaven's sake. I've got crow's-feet starting about my eyes, not to mention those horizontal creases across my throat that came out of nowhere, and my hands are starting to look lumpy around the knuckles of my skinny fingers. I've got a mortgage that is most of the way toward being paid off and my idea of a good evening is curling up in front of a *CSI* rerun on TV with a glass of port and a bag of low-sodium pretzels.

Yet when those two looked at me in my tie-dyed dress, they looked. I mean, with happy appreciation, like they were seeing right through the fabric. Or at least, I think they did. Maybe I was imagining it. Maybe it's the first sign of early menopause and I'm going batty.

Goddamn. It's been so long since any bloke fancied me. I'm letting this go to my head.

So I smile and sell ice cream and try hard not to think about them too often, though when I hear a siren going off somewhere I can't help wondering if they're on their way to the county hospital with some emergency. Heatstroke probably, in this weather. It's got to the point that I'm quite grateful to be working over the open freezer.

Then maybe an hour later, while I'm taking the opportunity during a lull to swig bottled water, I see an ambulance nosing through the crowd. The sirens are quiet this time. My stall is on the main avenue between the first aid point and the main arena, so I guess they are on their way down to do their demo. Matt is driving; I spot him through the windscreen as I wipe my lips with the back of my hand, and I feel a kick of shameful pleasure inside me. Suddenly the passenger door opens and Trev drops out, hustling through the crowd, heading straight for me. His dark eyes seize mine. Before I can think what to say, he snatches the big bottle of water from my hand and plants a hard peck on my cheek.

"Need this. Thanks, love," he says, hurrying back to the ambulance.

My face burns.

Elderflower: nature's champagne. It works well on the light, clean base of the sheep's milk, I think, though sometimes I make elderflower sorbet too. The tiny white flowers have to be plucked from the stalks of the flower head with a fork, and they go everywhere. I always end up with them in my hair, like tiny stars against my burning red, hennaed locks. I love elder, this humble everyday shrubby little tree with its sudden extravagant gift of perfumed blossom. I keep a careful watch on the best of the elder trees in the hedgerow down the lane behind my house, and make sure I pick at the perfect time. Get the wrong tree and you end up with the reek of cat pee. Get it right and you've got a fragrant note like pure joy.

I don't see the ambulance head back, but I might have missed it when I went off for my brief loo break, or I might just have been too busy with the queues. It's a hugely successful day; every one of my tubs is down to empty by the time the fête winds down. Well, nearly—I make sure I save enough for a couple of cones. As we hit the official closing time I take down the signs and clear up, padlocking the cashbox inside one of the freezers, stripping off the last set of plastic gloves and then washing and moisturizing my hands. It's the same routine as always, but this time I'm more on edge. I keep an eye out as I wipe down and pack up.

They don't show.

I don't let myself be disappointed; that would be an admission of something deeply foolish. Instead I make up two sugar cones with generous scoops of ice cream—one chocolate-and-chili, one honey-and-saffron—and I pop them in the plastic rack for holding cones and head up to the first aid point on foot. All around me stalls are being dismantled and vans loaded. I consider letting my hair down from its thick plait—I know my features are on the sharp side and loose hair softens them—but that's one step too far toward undignified.

At the first aid post the volunteers from the St. John's brigade are drinking tea and filling in forms. The ambulance is parked at the side of the tent, and I walk round it to the back. My mouth is dry; the potential for embarrassing myself here is immense.

There they are, at the back of the open vehicle, folding up the legs of a stretcher and loading it in.

"Still want those ice creams?" I ask brightly.

"Hey...Abbie!" The smiles seem genuine. Their interest in the ice cream certainly is: they both reach for the cones eagerly, bickering like boys over who gets the chocolate one. Trev volunteers for the honey, takes a big mouthful and then widens his eyes.

"Bloody Nora...this is good!"

"I know that." I allow myself to feel smug. My visit is vindicated.

"Have a seat, love," suggests Matt, indicating the back step of the ambulance. I sit myself down, and he instantly perches on my right. He's so close that I automatically attempt to shift up, but Trev is already on my left side, settling himself comfortably, one arm sweeping round behind my back. Not touching me, but definitely in my personal space. My sunburned upper arms brush their shirts.

I put my hands on my knees and laugh, only it comes out as a giggle. God, I'm acting like a teenager—or an idiot. "That's better. I've been on my feet all day."

"How did it go?" asks Matt.

"I sold every last scoop."

"So...what's your favorite flavor?" Trev wonders.

"These two," I answer honestly. "That's why I brought both; I can't choose between them." Then I catch his lifted eyebrows and blush. Matt, chuckling, offers me the chocolate cone.

"Want a lick?"

I shrug one shoulder and nod, tipping my lips to the creamy chocolate his tongue has already swirled over. Goddamn, we're flirting. How did this happen? What the hell do they see in me? I'm not ugly, okay—but I'm an artsy middle-aged lady who makes outrageous ice cream and wears clothes two decades old and her hair in a style and color that's too young for her. I'm not like them; not the sort of person who can press into a drunken crowd or a freezing pond to rescue someone from certain death, not the sort of person who can address a total stranger as "love." I haven't even worked for a living until recently—I went straight from art college into marriage, and the divorce settlement and child maintenance were generous enough to keep me and Skye living comfortably. I'm a joke, by their standards.

The chili heat burns on my tongue. My cheeks are already flushed. Matt grins at me, an easy wickedness dancing in his hazel eyes, as I lick my lips. I'm not trying to be provocative, honestly: you have to lick your lips if you are eating ice cream. "That's hot stuff," he teases.

"This is better," says Trev on my left. "Try some of this, Abbie." It would be rude not to, so I turn to the golden ice cream he offers. This one is melting faster: it's dribbling down the cone and threatening to slide off. I catch a big gobbet on my tongue, aware that they find my action vastly entertaining and still not quite believing it. "Bloody hell," says Trev happily.

"You like the taste of his cream better than mine?" Matt complains and I giggle. Then a cold drip hits my skin, and I realize the honey ice cream is dribbling out of the tip of the cone and is marking the front of my dress.

"Ack!" I yelp, half laughing, looking down. "Call myself a professional, eh?'

There's a drip on the inner curve of my left breast. I'm not wearing a bra—what would I need a bra for, after breast-feeding Skye flattened them so?—and this dress has a rather deep V-neck. The white trail winds down toward the cleft.

"Oh," says Trev, looking too. "Oh...that's..."

"Hold on," orders Matt. He drops his own ice cream back into the rack and then swiftly kneels before me. His fingertips graze my thighs. "Keep still," he commands. I feel Trev's free hand settle on the small of my back and my spine arches, thrusting my cleavage out a little more. Delicately—and it surprises me that this hearty, vital man is so careful—Matt leans forward until his lips are brushing my upper breast. I feel his breath on my skin: my own stops in my throat. I feel the tip of his tongue as he gently licks me clean.

My heart is pounding. The world seems to lurch. I stare over his head, wild eyed. We're tucked away here, shielded by the first aid tent. Sunlight glints on the dark leaves of the hedgerow and the discarded cans in the long grass. His lips are on my breast in a lingering kiss, causing my nipples to respond greedily, hardening to points. And Trev's hand slides up and down my spine, slow and firm.

Then Matt sits back. "Trev's right," he says softly, his eyes narrowing with hidden laughter. "That's bloody good."

Despite the warmth of the day, my nipples are standing up hard against the soft cotton. My sex is full of melting honey.

"Let's go inside, Abbie," Trev murmurs in my ear. "Come on."

Chocolate and Chili: oh, this is not the chocolate of childhood. This is a purely adult pleasure—bittersweet, dark and troubling. Heat lingering upon the lips and the breath. It is chocolate that makes the pupils dilate, the skin flush, the heart quicken. It is the taste of passion.

They take me into the ambulance and close the door on the outside world. I glance around—emergency equipment, foldout chairs, bright plastic drawers—but to be honest I'm not taking anything in. My brain has frozen. All I can think is that this is happening to me, and that I don't understand how. Is it a joke they're playing? Will they suddenly back off and start to laugh at me? Will they—?

They kiss me, both of them in turn, urging up against me with their big, hard bodies, sandwiching me between them as they press their caresses upon me. I taste chocolate and chili, honey and saffron. Their tongues are eager, their hands bold. Stubble scrapes my skin. Teeth tease my ears, my neck, my nipples. Trev has kept hold of his ice cream, though it is melting over his hand now: he encourages me to lick it, to suck his fingers, to pass the soft cream from my mouth to his. In the meantime Matt is pulling up my dress, working it over my shoulders, stripping me bare.

I tremble, anticipating their mockery.

Instead, the flash of Trev's teeth signals pure appetite. He touches the melting ice cream to my right nipple, and as I flinch from the cold Matt catches me, holding me still. As Matt props himself against the stretcher bed and pulls me off balance against him, Trev paints my body with the cold cream: my freckled breastbone, my dark stiff nipples, my puckered stomach. All the way down to the juncture of my legs. He tugs down my panties and, discarding the cone, squashes the last handful of ice cream into my sex, slathering it over my labia, squashing it up into my hot core until it melts and runs down my thighs. It's shudderingly cold and I squirm in Matt's embrace, biting back the squeals. I'm half aware that the blond man is tugging at his own clothes, pulling his cock out, but I can't see it—I just know it as a slab of burning heat thrust against my cold bottom.

Then Trev gets down and eats the ice cream off me, tits and belly and thighs, all the way. I must be salty from the day's work but he doesn't care. His mouth is both hungry and tender. It makes me fear, and it makes me need, and ultimately it makes me surrender, opening my legs to let him plunge his mouth and his hand between. His fingers go inside me, diving through the cream. His mouth devours my clit, sucking and nibbling and licking like I'm a gelato. I heave up against Matt's torso, feeling his hands cup my breasts and tug at my sticky nipples. I'm helpless to resist. Trev's hand is working me insistently, each thrust opening me more. His mouth has taken control of my whole body. Matt's tongue is hot and wet in my ear; I'm being eaten by both men and I can't stop it, I can't help it, I'm coming now with breathy unmistakable squeals—and Matt growls "Yes— you give it all up now; that's right," in my ear as my world turns inside out.

Orgasm leaves me shaken and trembling. Trev stands and pulls me up against him, stroking the wet strands of hair back from my face, and I focus my eyes with some effort. He's smiling, but his cock is straining impatiently against me. I can feel it through his green paramedic trousers. "What happens now?" I ask in a tiny voice.

"What do you want to happen, Abbie?" he murmurs, brushing my face with kisses, rubbing my palm against the swollen ridge in his pants.

"I want..." I reach behind me for Matt. He's got his flies open and his cock is standing up hard under his stroking hand, and as he guides my fingers to grip that thick shaft I realize he's already clad it in a skin of latex. Smooth operator.

"Want this?" Matt asks, voice full of chocolate.

"I want both of you," I confess.

Trev's eyebrows arch. "Together?'

What am I thinking of, at my age? This is crazy. "Yes," I gasp.

Trev nods, and hands me back to Matt like a gift. He pulls me into his lap, tipping me forward from the hips to get the right angle. I spread my thighs, groaning involuntarily as I feel his blunt cockhead press home into the wild sweet slather of my pussy. I tip farther down, looking up, and I glimpse his ruddy, golden-furred balls bouncing between my thighs as he works his way inside me with little jiggling thrusts. It feels wonderful—and my long-unused muscles are responding to his girth as if to a miracle. I'm turning from solid to liquid. But I'm so off balance I'm going to fall, and I reach out and grab Trev's thighs to steady myself.

He's unbuttoning his shirt and unbuckling his belt. He reveals a flat stomach furred with dark hair and a long stiff cock that's already slick at the tip. Taking my head by my braided hair, he feeds that member between my lips. His cock and balls taste salty, sweaty and sexual—it would make a terrible flavor for an ice cream, and I'm so hungry for it.

The ambulance is cramped, our positions lacking all grace. I'm glad I don't have to do much except hold on in there. Matt thrusts into my pussy and Trev fucks my throat. I give him a swirling lick with my tongue on each backstroke but my concentration is already slipping elsewhere; as I reach down to my own clit, feeling the tendons tighten in my legs, I know I'm going to hit orgasm again, this time with both men inside me, my throat and pussy both full of cock and semen and ice cream.

"I'm coming," gasps Trev.

Honey and Saffron: I make my own blend of honeys, not too sharp and not so mild that it's dulled by the cold. There has to be a fragrance that hits with every mouthful. But it's the saffron that makes it addictive: warm, sumptuous, tantalizing saffron. Tasting like sunlight on summer hay, it is the most expensive spice in the world, and the balm for every hurting heart.

ABOUT THE AUTHORS

VALERIE ALEXANDER is a freelance writer and novelist living in Arizona. Her work has been published in *Best of Best Women's Erotica* and *Best Lesbian Erotica*.

JACQUELINE APPLEBEE (writing-in-shadows.co.uk) is a black, bisexual British woman who breaks down barriers with smut. Jacqueline's stories have appeared in anthologies including *Best Women's Erotica, Best of Best Women's Erotica 2,* and *Best Lesbian Erotica.* Jacqueline has penned *Erotic Brits,* a sexy tour around the United Kingdom and Ireland.

JANINE ASHBLESS (janineashbless.blogspot.com) is the author of five books of paranormal and fantasy erotica published by Black Lace and blogs about minotaurs, Victorian art and writing dirty. Her short stories for Cleis have been published in anthologies including *Best Women's Erotica 2009, Sweet Love* and *Fairy Tale Lust.*

Located somewhere in the wilds of the Delmarva Peninsula, **CHRISSIE BENTLEY** is the author of seven erotic novels and collections, and myriad short stories, published online and in print. An avid collector of vintage erotic film and photographs, she has three cats and a sense of humor.

RACHEL KRAMER BUSSEL (rachelkramerbussel.com) is an author, editor, blogger and In the Flesh Reading Series host. Her books include the novel *Everything But* and the nonfiction work *The Art of the Erotic Love Letter*. She's edited over thirty erotica anthologies, including *Passion; Fast Girls; Spanked; Peep Show; Please, Sir* and *Please, Ma'am*.

LANA FOX is a writing instructor and assistant magazine editor. Her erotic stories have appeared, or are forthcoming, in Clean Sheets and anthologies published by Xcite Books, Harlequin Spice and Cleis Press. She also publishes literary and fantasy fiction under a different name. Find Lana online at: lanafox.com.

CYNTHIA HAMILTON is the pen name of a bisexual woman living in San Francisco. By day, she edits fiction professionally. After hours, she likes to let her own imagination off the leash.

LOUISA HARTE's (louisaharte.com) erotic fiction appears in the Cleis Press anthologies *Best Women's Erotica 2010* and *Fairy Tale Lust*. Currently living in New Zealand, she finds inspiration from many places, including her thoughts, dreams and fantasies.

LOUISE LAGRIS lives in New York City and likes it very much most of the time.

KIRSTY LOGAN (kirstylogan.com) has only been to Skye once, but now dreams of islands. She writes, edits, teaches and reviews books in Glasgow, Scotland. Her first erotic short story is published in *Girl Crush,* and her nonfiction sex writing appears at The Rumpus and Clean Sheets. She has a semicolon tattooed on her toe.

Author of hundreds of short dirty stories, **SOMMER MARSDEN** (SmutGirl.blogspot.com) has appeared in dozens of anthologies, and she is the author of numerous novels including the upcoming *Calendar Girl.* Sommer recently edited some stellar authors in *Dirtyville* and *Kinkyville* for her own so small it's nearly invisible press, Spastic Girl Press.

VELVET MOORE (VelvetMoore.com) is a twentysomething who began writing erotica-style works during adolescence and officially entered the world of erotic fiction several years ago. She has been published on the Web at sites including CleanSheets. com and TheEroticWoman.com, and ForTheGirls.com. She currently resides in Ohio.

LOLA OLSON is a soon to be grad student grateful for sex positivity as it's made a positive influence in her life. She has gone from hating her body and fearing sexuality to embracing it and using it positively.

GISELLE RENARDE is the author of over a dozen books and a short story contributor to more than twenty. For more information on Giselle Renarde and her work, visit her website at freewebs.com/giscllerenarde.

DONNA GEORGE STOREY (DonnaGeorgeStorey.com) is the author of *Amorous Woman,* a very steamy tale of an American woman's love affair with Japan. Her erotic fiction has been published in numerous anthologies including *Best Women's Erotica, Best American Erotica* and *X: The Erotic Treasury.*

CECILIA TAN (blog.ceciliatan.com) is the author of many, many books and erotic short stories, including *White Flames, Black Feathers, Mind Games, Edge Plays* and *Telepaths Don't Need Safewords.* Her erotic stories have appeared in such far-flung and disparate places as *Ms.* magazine, *Asimov's Science Fiction Magazine, Best American Erotica, Nerve,* and *Penthouse.* She is the founder and editorial director of Circlet Press.

AMELIA THORNTON is a very good girl with very bad thoughts who lives by the English seaside with her collection of school canes, a lot of vintage lingerie, and too many shoes. She enjoys baking, hard spankings and writing beautiful naughtiness.

ALYSSA TURNER's writings address a woman's desire to really have it all—including the things she's not supposed to want. New to the erotica scene, Alyssa has enjoyed a career in art and design, and enjoys painting pictures with a creative use of metaphor and detailed visual imagery. She lives in New York with her husband and son.

ALISON TYLER in an insomniac pornographer who has spent the past two decades writing dirty stories and naughty novels, editing erotic anthologies, and drinking massive amounts of caffeine. Her latest antho is *Alison's Wonderland.* She serves coffee and snark 24/7 at alisontyler.blogspot.com.

VIOLET BLUE (tinynibbles.com, @violetblue) is a *Forbes* "Web Celeb" and one of *Wired*'s "Faces of Innovation"—in addition to being a blogger, high-profile tech personality and infamous podcaster. Violet also has many award-winning, best-selling books; an excerpt from her *Smart Girl's Guide to Porn* is featured on Oprah Winfrey's website. She is regarded as the foremost expert in the field of sex and technology, a sex-positive pundit in mainstream media (CNN, *The Oprah Winfrey Show, The Tyra Banks Show*) and is regularly interviewed, quoted and featured prominently by major media outlets. A published feature writer and columnist since 1998, she also writes for media outlets such as *MacLife, O: The Oprah Magazine* and the UN-sponsored international health organization RH Reality Check. She was the notorious sex columnist for the *San Francisco Chronicle* with her weekly column "Open Source Sex." She headlines at conferences ranging from ETech, LeWeb and SXSW: Interactive, to Google Tech Talks at Google, Inc. The *London Times* named Blue "one of the 40 bloggers who really count."